13.99

AF699749

FOUR WINDS ACROSS TEXAS

volume one

FOUR WINDS ACROSS TEXAS

BY DR. TIM R. MASON

DISCARD

Tate Publishing & *Enterprises*

HURST PUBLIC LIBRARY

Four Winds Across Texas
Copyright © 2008 by Dr. Tim R. Mason. All rights reserved.

This title is also available as a Tate Out Loud product. Visit www.tatepublishing.com for more information.

No part of this publication may be reproduced, stored in a retrieval system or transmitted in any way by any means, electronic, mechanical, photocopy, recording or otherwise without the prior permission of the author except as provided by USA copyright law.

The opinions expressed by the author are not necessarily those of Tate Publishing, LLC.

Published by Tate Publishing & Enterprises, LLC
127 E. Trade Center Terrace | Mustang, Oklahoma 73064 USA
1.888.361.9473 | www.tatepublishing.com

Tate Publishing is committed to excellence in the publishing industry. The company reflects the philosophy established by the founders, based on Psalm 68:11,
"The Lord gave the word and great was the company of those who published it."

Book design copyright © 2008 by Tate Publishing, LLC. All rights reserved.
Cover design by Lynly Taylor
Interior design by Jonathan Lindsey

Published in the United States of America

ISBN: 978-1-60604-129-1

1. Fiction: Western: General

08.03.18

Dedication

This work is affectionately dedicated to my late wife of fifty years, Bettie Louise Justice, of Noodle, Texas, and our three children, Jacque Lynn Mason Rogers and husband, Gary, of Quanah, Texas; Judy Ann Mason Cornutt and husband, Jim, of New York City; and Jeff Alan Mason and wife, Jenna, of Coppell, Texas.

Grateful acknowledgement goes to Bettie's late parents, V.R. and Wanna Justice, of Merkel, Texas, and to their other two children, Bettie's sister, Maxine Justice Poplin, and husband, Bill, of Houston, Texas; and brother, Roy Justice and wife, Nancy, of Olmito, Texas.

Mr. Justice served as a church elder for many years, and

so did his son and both sons-in-law, all in the Church of Christ.

All these played a big part in making my life a great ride.

Tim R. (Doc) Mason

Chapter 1

I had never seen my dad cry before. He wasn't a big, strong, and handsome man, but he was my dad, and me and my little brother, Toby, sure did like him. He worked from sunup to sundown, or as Granpaw used to say, "From can to can't." But Dad liked to fish and tell us stories about him and Uncle Barlow and Granpaw when they lived in the hills of east Tennessee.

When me and Toby come around the back of the barn, there was Dad kinda leanin' aginst the barn sittin' on a bundle of feed that was on the ground. I didn't say anythin' about him sittin' on the feed, even tho' me and Toby had worked all one day last week puttin' the bundles into shocks, and here was Dad with one of 'em on the ground. I guess the feelin' in the pit of my innards kep' me from sayin' anythin'. Toby was three years younger'n me, and a fourteen-year-old sometimes don't have the sense of a green gourd about things like that, and Toby lit into 'im about messin' up our shock and him cryin' and all.

Well, Dad wiped his eyes dry on his shirt sleeves and took me and Toby by our shoulders, and we all sat down and Dad told us about Mom. 'Course, I wasn't too surprised since I was seventeen and knowed all year that Mom wasn't too good and didn't work much like she did 'fore she got sick. Dad said Doc Hanley was in the house all day with Mom and that was why he didn't come fishin' with us like he said he would. Likely, Mom would not live more'n a day or two.

"Why, Dad?" Toby asked. "Was it cause me and Jeff was mean to her and not doin' our chores like she wanted us to?"

"No, son. Doc says her body is jist plum wore out from the consumption."

"But can't we find somethin' to hep her, or git another doctor to make her well?" Toby asked again.

"No, son. Doc is doin' all he can. The neighbor ladies is all there. She jist can't breathe normal."

I asked if me and Toby could go talk to her, and he said yes, so we started to the house, but Mrs. Granby came out bawlin' and Dad and me knew it was too late. Toby looked at me as Mrs. Granby came and hugged Dad and they both cried. Then they came to us and took us both bawlin' into the house.

I'll never forget the feeling I had when Toby and me saw Dad kneel down and tenderly kiss Mom's face and hold her hand to his face. Toby and me went to her bed and held her hand for the last time. I wanted to run hide in the barn loft, but I knew Dad needed me to act growed up and look after Toby, so we all went into the other room while they fixed Mom up for the buryin'.

Folks from miles around musta heard about Mom bein'

sick and dyin', 'cause they started comin' and bringin' food like I'd never seen before. It looked like a camp meetin', especially when the preacher from the Church of Christ over in Ashdown came with his wife and three kids, one of them bein' Julie Benton, age sixteen, who was as pretty as a newborn doe. Any other time I'd've delighted in playin' tricks on her like me and Bud Hinton did the time we put some tree-gum in her desk seat at school and nearly ruint her new dress. But not today. It was not the right time for that kind of stuff.

They musta been two hunnert or more at Mom's funeral. They was standin' all around the new grave in Pine Hill Cemetery. I didn't know that Brother Benton knowed my mom so good, but he talked a long time about how good she was, and me and Toby was real proud, 'cept it didn't make us feel so good when we realized they was gettin' ready to put her in that hole.

Well, I done pretty good at actin' growed up 'til they lowered the box and folks started comin' by and huggin' me and shakin' my hand and sayin' things like, "Poor Toby and Jeff. What's to become of you boys?" Seems to me like they thought we was goin' to the dogs or maybe we was goin' to die too since Mom was gone.

I'll tell a man, Julie cried a lot too. When she took my hand and hugged my neck, I got that funny feelin' in my stomach again. Only this time it was different. I nearly died. I shore hoped Bud wasn't lookin', but he was and he was cryin' too. So maybe it would be all right, and I busted out cryin' again.

★

In the year that passed following Mom's buryin', Dad spent as much time as possible with me and Toby. Tom said, "You boys need to stay with yore book learnin' all you can. They ain't nothin' I can teach you boys since I can't hardly read none myself. The day's comin' when a man'll need all he can learn. This farm ain't big enough to pay you both a livin', so learn all you can at school."

He made us read to him most every night by lamp. We didn't know it, but he was learnin' too. I didn't figure that out for a long time. I also figured out that time was a good healer. The pain of Mom bein' gone didn't hurt as much anymore. Me and Toby shore got closer to Dad that year.

Once we had a great time. It was in the spring. The winter had been very rough, and feed was scarce for our cows, and we all spent long hours helpin' the animals through the winter. Several calves were born dead or died from the scours and lung fever after bein' born. The losses would be hard to make up, and money would be scarce again. But that ain't what I started to tell you.

Spring finally come, and the grass was growin' so things started perkin' up. So did our spirits. One night Dad told us about how his Dad and older brother used to go grapplin' for catfish on the Little River when they was young boys.

Toby asked, "How do you know where the fish are?"

"Well, you don't really know. But if you are kinda brave and adventuresome, you'll find 'em."

"But how, Dad? Is the water clear enough to see the fish?"

I interrupted Toby to remind him of the time we waded in the Little River while we was chasin' a coon.

"You could see clear to the bottom and it was over twelve foot deep in places."

"Shore," Dad said. "I've been in holes too deep to touch bottom and nearly run out of air tryin' to get to the top. Fact is, your Uncle Barlow most nearly had his arm tore off by a catfish that musta weighed nigh on to forty pounds."

"Reck'n we could go sometime, Dad?" I asked.

"Sure thing. Tomorrow we'll go see Lukey Travers and git him to make us a big hook like a fish hook, only bigger. Now you boys read your Bible for a while and then we'll say our prayers and go to bed. Looks like tomorrow is gonna be a big day."

"Sure does," we echoed in unison.

I turned to the Book of Jonah and the story of him and the whale that God had prepared. Somehow the story took on a new meaning as I read to Toby and got in mind to grapple for a big fish of our own. Dad came in before I finished reading, and he listened to me read. Then he prayed for the good times we had when Mom was alive and hoped that someway she could be along when we fished tomorrow.

Later I heard Dad praying again, and he asked God to help him take good care of me and Toby and to make good men of us. What he did not know was that me and Toby had been thinkin' the same thing. Somewhere the Good Book said, "The effectual fervent prayer of a righteous man availeth much."

I didn't know what some of them words meant, but I knew Dad was a righteous man, and it had to be talkin' about him.

Long before the sun came up, me and Toby finished our chores. It was Saturday and no school, so after eating we raced to see who could saddle up first. I usually won because I was taller and stronger, but that day Toby won.

"See. I told you I'd win. You jist don't spend enough time with yore horse, Jeff."

"Well, okay fer you, but I'm savin' up fer the biggest fish. You wait an' see, Toby."

"Since you lost, you got to saddle up Dad's horse."

"I would, but look around an' tell me where it's at. He left here an hour ago, and look, here he comes now up the trail."

"Where you been to, Dad?" Toby asked.

"I took some eggs over to the Bentons."

"Did you see Julie?" I asked. "I ain't seen her much lately at school."

But then Toby started callin' me taffy leg 'cause I was sweet on Julie, and Dad had to call him off before we got in a fight.

"Julie said tell you hello and if we caught some fish, she and Mrs. Benton would cook for us at their house at dinner tomorrow after church."

"Hooray!" I shouted.

"Bah," Toby said.

It took Lukey Travers about an hour to heat the rod, shape it, and file the point like a real fish hook. It had a long rod about three foot on the other end.

"Here 'tis, boys. Be real kearful and don't hook a leg. It'll hev to be cut off."

"Thanks, Mr. Travers. How much we owe?" I asked.

"Nuthin'. Jist bring me a mess of fish sometime."

"Gee willikers, thanks, sir," Toby said as we headed for the door.

Toby and me had jist mounted up when Dad said, "Look, boys, that man comin' here is William Story, the greatest bear hunter in all of Arkansas. Let's wait and maybe talk to him."

We were excited. You never seen such boys as us. Well, Mr. Story wasn't taken with too many words, but he did invite me and Toby to his camp sometime and he'd tell us a tale or two about bear huntin'. We promised to come see him soon.

★

We didn't have time to make it clear to Little River, but Mr. Story had told us about a good fishin' hole called Walnut Bayou. We got there after about an hour an' started unpackin' our gear, not that it amounted to very much.

The water was flowing rapidly to the south where it would wind up in the Red River. Dad had tied a rope to all of us in case somebody stepped in a washout or if we slipped and fell. About 30 foot from where we entered the water, some large rocks was stickin' up.

"Here we are, boys. Let's try this place," Dad said. He was only waist deep, but Toby was in deeper since he wasn't as tall. Dad began feeling around the biggest rock with his feet and the hook. Soon he found a hole going under the rock at the bottom where the sand shifted. He told me to stand there while he went all around the rock.

"No more holes," he said. "Now if a fish is in there, he has to come out this hole."

Now come the hard part. Dad would take a deep breath, go under the water, and poke the straight end of the rod in the hole and try to feel a fish. On the fourth try he come up and said he thought one was in there.

We was gittin' kinda chilled, but I didn't dare to complain 'cause it was excitin' and fun. Then Dad said, "The dangerous way to git 'em is to reach in there and stick yore hand into the gills and out their mouth. That's what happened when yore Uncle Barlow near got his arm tore off. That fish jist clamped down and took off, draggin' pore Bud under and in circles. The fish went under a limb in the water, and Bud hung on it and his arm scraped near to the bone as it come out of the mouth of that fish."

"Boy, that's not fer me," Toby said.

"Me neither," I added.

"Well, that's when William Story told us about this hook

idea he had. He used it all the time. It's much safer," Dad said. "What you do is learn the feel of pokin' the rod or stick in the mud or sand or rock. After that, when you feel something different, it's probably a fish. If he's small, he jist might move over a bit or dart out of the hole. If he's big, he can't move very far, so he shifts a little. If the hook is poked near his head, he gits a little mad and tries to bite it. You can tell if he clamps down on it. Then you brace real good and jerk the rod. This sets the hook in his mouth. Then the hard work begins."

"What do you mean hard work, Dad? Won't he jist come out?" Toby asked.

"Well, if he's a five-pounder he might, but his fins are sharp and he wriggles to git loose, so you have to hold him away from yore legs. That's why we have a long metal rod. If he's big, like a ten- or twenty-pounder, it takes muscle to hold him. It's a good idea to poke a rope through his gills and out his mouth and tie it tight and have a long enough rope in case he gits loose or you drop the rod. So, git the rope ready."

I did.

It took a few minutes of pokin' and probin', but finally Dad, who was kinda tired and winded from bein' underwater so many times, said, "Here goes," and under he went. The fish musta bit the hook 'cause Dad jerked out and up and come up fer air.

"Here, Jeff, grab hold the rod and hand me the rope."

We both pulled, and then Toby got hold of the rod with me and the catfish come to the edge of the rock hole. Dad went under agin and poked the rope through the gills and out the mouth and tied it tight. Then we pulled the rod and Dad pulled the rope.

Well, I can tell you what a fin feels like in a leg 'cause

he got me good when he come out, and it ain't quit hurtin' yet, but I didn't let on much. We drug him to the bank, and he musta weighed near on to eight to ten pounds. It took a while fer us to git warm, but we went back and me and Toby got to grapple, and sure enough, Toby got two and I got one, and his were both bigger'n mine.

"I told you so," he said.

"Yep," I replied. "But I'll git you next time.

I gave my six-pounder to Mr. Travers fer makin' the hook, but not 'til after we cleaned and dressed it, 'cause Dad said that's more neighborly. I really think he meant to say it's more Christian. Anyways, Mr. Travers had some good catfish, and we still had the hook. Pretty good trade, I'd say. The rest of the fish we cleaned to take to the Bentons fer Sunday dinner. I was sure hungry to go, but not fer the reason Toby was.

Chapter 2

Brother Benton preached fer about an hour, and them that didn't git preached into hell wished they was already there. Boy, he really was wound up tight. I guess his gittin' finished perked me up considerable, 'cause I was sure ready to ride with Julie to their farm.

Miz Benton and Julie gabbed all the way 'bout how pretty the day was and the flowers and trees and all. Brother Benton and Dad was busy talking cattle talk and growin' hay. That left me and Toby with nothin' except to talk fishin' and stuff, which we did.

"What you boys been doin' of late?" Brother Benton asked.

"Workin' and loafin'," I replied.

"Yeah," Toby said. "I'm workin', Jeff's loafin."

That got a laugh from everybody but me, and Julie said, "Sounds just like you, you loafer."

"I'll git you fer that, and you too, Toby. Jist wait and see."

Well, the fish meal really was good, and Miz Benton had a bunch of fixin's to go with the fish. We stuffed enough in to last a month at least.

"Toby, you and Jeff come with me to the barn. Tab is down there fixing a crate for the setting hen," Julie said. Tab was the son of the black family that worked for the Benton's and he was about Jeff's age. So we went out and follered her. At least Toby follered her. Me, I jist walked right beside her so I could nearly touch her. She was so pretty, with her blonde hair and copper skin. She looked lovely, and every time I thought about her I could feel a blush comin' on.

The barn was nearly two hundred yards away, and I never could understand a body buildin' a barn so far from the house. It was a long walk on cold or rainy days.

"Help! Help!"

And with that loud shout, the barn door banged open and Tab came running out lickety-split, his eyes buggin' out, and the hair on my neck must've stood straight up.

"Snake! Snake!" he yelled.

"Did it bite?" I hollered.

"No. I didn't give it a chanct."

By that time he had stopped runnin' and we found out what happened.

Tab said, "I put some hay in the crate and moved a bale to git some more loose hay and there was these two snakes. Man, I dropped the hay and lit out."

"Julie, where's the hoe? We can git them and cut off their rattles. Were they rattlers, Tab?" Toby asked.

"I didn't take time to look. But I ain't goin' back in there."

"You're a sissy coward, Tab, if you don't," Julie said.

If I had called Tab names like that he'd a-skinned me, but Julie got the hoe and gave it to me. Toby and Tab carefully moved the bale of hay and saw the two snakes. Fer the next few minutes, excitement was high. Finally, we got both of 'em. They were not rattlers but the deadly and beautiful coral snakes with red and yellow and gold rings around their bodies.

"Red and yeller kill a feller," I said.

"Not me," Tab said.

I don't blame him fer bein' scared. It reminded me of the time he was gatherin' eggs and the layin' hens had nests up about six feet high stacked up on each other. Tab was only about twelve then and had to stand on tippy-toes and reach up to the top nest and feel fer the eggs.

One day, he reached up and felt fer the egg and his finger felt kinda wet, so thinkin' he was feelin' a broken egg, without movin' his hand, he stood on a box and raised up to git the egg. He saw his finger stickin' down the mouth of a large snake. They nearly had to build a new barn, and the white folks almost got a new member right then.

Lucky fer Tab, it was not a poisonous snake and was harmless, but you can see why Tab don't like snakes.

We helped him finish the settin' nest and put eighteen eggs under the old settin' hen. We all looked to the time of hatchin' and seein' a bunch of new baby chicks in about three weeks. Maybe with the snakes gone, the chicks would make it if the skunks and coons and foxes didn't come around. Tab would be there to help out, anyway.

Pa and Brother Benton came to the barn to see what the commotion was about. They patted us on the back too. Toby had actually killed them, the snakes, not Pa and Brother Benton. We gave him the praise, even though me and Tab had done the risky part. Julie had stood up about three rungs on the ladder to the hayloft, so she had a little excitement, but not as much as us. But, considerin' she's a girl, I guess that was a lot.

Chapter 3

About a week after my eighteenth birthday, William Story came by and asked if me and Toby wanted to go bear huntin'. Dad said cold as it was we'd better wear some clothes instead of goin' bare, but he's always pokin' fun at us, and we let him 'cause he's such a good dad.

Anyway we did, and boy, what a time we had. There ain't a better woodsman in all the world than Mr. Story, and that includes Robin Hood and the deer slayer we read about in school.

Well, the Bentons were rich compared to us and could afford a maid who was really supposed to be a slave, but Mr. Benton, being a preacher, he agreed with Alexander Campbell that slavery wasn't condemned in the book, but slaves were not to be mistreated. Mr. Benton had a black woman about forty years old whose man had either been sold away or killed, and she had a boy named Tablet (maybe named after one of Moses' tablets of commandments). He was older than Toby, but younger than me by about two months. They worked on the Benton farm, and Tablet, he kinda looked after Julie and kept other boys from making over her too much. I guess I should've told about Tab earlier, but I forgot.

Tablet was another six-footer like me and strong as an ox. He went everywhere we did when he didn't have to work. Mr. Benton let him go bear huntin', so William Story, Toby, Tab, and me took the road north out of Willow Springs that leads up to Anderson's Ferry on Little River. The trip took about seven hours by horseback.

Mr. Anderson had talked with some men who had come downriver from Cerro Gordo. They reported that several bear were seen in the area of Jones Farm up in Indian Territory. Most of the Caddo Indians had gone to a reservation, and only a few Choctaws were still living in the territory.

We found a good place to make camp about two miles south of Cerro Gordo. Mr. Story didn't want us to go into town because the roughest element of people lived there. He didn't want us to get hurt, especially Tablet. One of the meanest men in the south was a slave trader who would even resort to stealin' another man's slaves, sellin' off the men and beddin' down the girls, especially the young ones, before he sold them. Me'n Toby had heard Dad and Mom talk about that one night, so we knew what it was all about.

Tab was very excited when the name of Slave Trader Morton was mentioned. Morton was probably the man who sold Tab's pa.

"Well now, let's git some vittles into our hollow bellies and git ready fer tomorrow," Story said.

"What kin ah do?" Tab asked. "Cook or put up the tent?"

"You cook. We'll put up the tent," Story replied.

Tab prepared a meal of meat, potatoes, sliced onions, and sourdough biskits. I drank three cups of hot coffee, which would probably keep me up half the night to get relief, but I didn't care. I could hardly sleep anyway, thinkin' about the bears, Slave Trader Morton ... and Julie.

We had a good sleep in the tent and broke camp at daybreak. Mr. Story and Tab had fixed eatin's early, so we were on our way. We passed a small Caddo settlement that stayed there and didn't go to the reservation. They were farmers and had a corn crop growin'. Their houses were made of long posts set in the ground in a circle and tied together at the top, and a thick grass cover was applied.

Story talked to one of the men, and he said a bear had killed two dogs the day before and almost killed a young girl before the men could git her away. The bear had three arrows in him as he left camp.

We went the directions they told us. In about a half hour, Story picked up his trail and showed us how to tell prints of walkin' from runnin'. One hind footprint was unusual and was probably caused by an arrow in the leg. The print was not as deep and was smeared like a foot was draggin' instead of bein' lifted.

In a few minutes Story said, "Here's two more sets of prints."

"What are they?" Toby asked.

"Two young cubs. Probably belong to her. Be watchful now. She'll be mean if we git her riled up. 'Specially with her wound and baby cubs."

Toby yelled, "There they are!" and his loud piercing voice caused the bears to run for more cover. The three dogs let us know right quick they knew what was goin' on. So, off we went, 'til I tripped on a root an' sprawled headlong into a clump of bushes. Thorny ones too. I almost said "hellfire" but caught myself jist in time. Tab pulled me up and we went on. Them thorns dealt me misery all day, but bears were more important, I thought.

The dogs had little trouble stayin' with the bear since she was losin' blood. Just when we were about to stop and rest, the dogs began barkin' real loud, so we closed in. Much to our surprise, the bears had disappeared, but I saw why. Just behind a large bush like I had dove into earlier, there was an opening to a cave. The dogs were running into and out of the opening and howling loud.

"Boys, I reck'n we got a bear or two," Story drawled.

"How we gonna git 'em out?" Toby asked.

That kinda bothered me too. I didn't want to go into a cave I didn't know and whip three bears and drag 'em out. But I didn't think Mr. Story would do that.

"Set a spell, boys. Them bears will stay put a while with them dogs there. We kin rest and plan a while."

That shore sounded good to us, so we streched out and rested and drunk some water from our canteens. We decided to build us a fire and heat some coffee, and Mr. Story suggested getting a pine knot on fire and holding it inside the cave for a look. The dogs got excited every time we came close.

According to Mr. Story, we were about a mile from Cerro Gordo, which was on a high bluff above us. The property we were on belonged to a Mr. Pauley, and the cave we found was called the Pauley Cave.

When we lit our pine knot torches and later explored the cave (after we got the bears out), we found it was not a cave, but a tunnel about six feet wide, six feet high, and about seventy feet long with a hole on the north end and two small holes on the south end.

We decided to wait 'til morning to take on the bears. I

sure was glad. It was too dark in the cave and the mama bear wounded and all. I think Tab and Toby was just as glad. Anyway, we slept good while the dogs watched the cave opening.

We woke to the smell of coffee and jumped up to help Mr. Story rustle up some breakfast. He had already checked the cave, and the bears were in the back part away from the dogs.

"Sure seems like a good day," he said.

Tab was ready to learn bear hunting and remarked, "I'm a bear hugger. Show me to 'em."

Toby laughed and said, "Bear hugger, my eye! I bet you'll be the last in the cave." Tab grinned and rolled his eyes and we all had a big laugh.

We lit the pine knots and Mr. Story and me took the rifles, and Tab and Toby each took a dog on a leash, and we slowly made our way into the cave. We had only gone about ten feet when Mr. Story stopped and we saw a crack in the west wall of the cave. He poked a light through and saw a small area like a little room. It was empty. We went on into the cave. The dogs were growling and barking, and there was a lot of racket in the back of the cave.

All of a sudden, I saw a beam of light coming in back of the cave. It was a small hole opening to the outside. We decided somebody needed to go out and find the hole and guard it. Tab volunteered, and Toby went with two dogs and a gun for protection.

After they found the opening, they yelled and the bears jumped at the noise. I thought they might come at us, but they stayed back. The dog we had was really tearing at the leash, and it was all I could do to hold him. Just then, Mr. Story saw the mama bear pushing a cub into a crevice. He yelled to Tab and Toby. It was another hole a few feet from them. They hadn't seen it, but when warned they set the dog onto the cub and it backed into the cave.

Mr. Story could see enough to take aim on the mama bear and put a bullet through her brain. She had lost so much blood it didn't take her long to die. Then two more shots took care of the cubs.

Well, the day was shorely exciting. We learned how to skin and scrape the hides. Boy, was the mama hide heavy. It weighed pert near seventy-five pounds. Mr. Story showed us how to quarter the carcass and save the best parts of meat. We buried the wasted parts, and Toby and Tab got the cub hides and I got the mama bear hide. I knew Julie would like it for a rug when it got cured out.

It took us most of the day to fix the meat, hides, and clean up everything. Before dark I took Tab and we went into the cave to look around.

Tab yelled, "Look out! I'se out of here!" He was really scared. Mr. Story and Toby ran in to see what it was. We found some human bones and skulls in the small room. Probably some Indian or early explorers, but it was gruesome.

There was some old pine knots that had been used for torches, and I found a piece of iron about ten inches long and covered with brass on one end.

Mr. Story said, "Looks like an old muzzle-loading flint lock pistol. Clean it up and it'll make a good keepsake to remind me of the bear hunt."

"I'll do it and remember this day 'til I'm dead."

The last thing we did was learn to cook bear meat. The meal was really tasty, especially since we worked so hard for it. We also slept good that night. So did the dogs. They were well- fed on bear meat.

Chapter 4

We left the bearskins and all our camp stuff in the cave and headed for Cerro Gordo. Mr. Story had to see a friend there about a trip to Colorado they had planned. He cautioned us to stay together and not go into any saloons. There were five in town. There was also a "pleasure house" we found out about but dared not go in. However, we walked by and looked at it from across the road but didn't see anything.

We walked around town looking at everything. They had a newspaper printing place and a barbershop and a bath house. The biggest place was the Mercantile Store. We all went in and wished on a lot of things.

I saw a buckskin jacket and pants and really wanted them, so I started planning on how I could save up eight dollars to buy them. Tab had to stay outside because he wasn't white. While he was standing outside, some rough-looking men walked up and held a gun on him and wanted to know who he slaved for.

"Hold on there, men. I'll handle this. Who are you, boy?" This was a man who had a star on his vest. He must've been the sheriff, and we quit worrying about Tab.

"I'm Tab, suh. I slave fer Mr. Benson," Tab answered.

"Yuh mean that do-gooder over at Ashdown?"

"Yes, suh, only I'm a free nigger."

"They ain't no sich thing as free niggers. Hossback, run fetch Morton. We got us a big boy."

"Yes, sir, Mr. Hasby. I'll git him."

The crowd got bigger and noisy. Me and Toby got scared, but we stood by Tab who was wide-eyed and sweating. I guess he was worried too.

Then a big, bald, mean-looking man with a handlebar mustache came walking up to Tab. He was carrying a long coiled whip.

"Who are you, boy? Stand up straight and let me see you. I claim you as mine, since you say you are free."

"My name is Tab an' my father was Moses Alexander an' I'm slave to Mr. Benton."

"I know that name, Moses Alexander. Sold him to a rich landholder man in South Texas. Got one thousand dollars fer him, an' you look like you're as good as him. Turn him around, Hasby, let's look at him an' see how sound he is."

"Make him strip!" yelled the man next to the Sheriff. I'd never saw any of this kind of action before and it made me sick to my stomach, like when Ma died.

Mr. Story and the newspaper man came up. Mr. Story had his long gun and he said, "Turn Tab loose, Morton."

Morton looked at the sheriff and back at the rifle in Story's hand. Getting no support from the sheriff, he said, "You'll rue this day, Story."

"Sheriff, this man is a free man, and I'll die before I let Morton touch him. That goes fer now" Mr. Story said.

The sheriff was convinced and said, "Nothin' to me. Git on an' go."

We all went and ate some of the food we brought from camp. Later, as we were about to leave Cerro Gordo, we heard a great commotion in the Red Dog Saloon. The loud, angry voice of Slave Trader Morton came booming out into the street.

"Hey, you skinny Mex, what ye doin' up here away from Mexico? Git back aginst thet wall an' drop thet frog sticker or I'll send a ball of lead thru ye."

The man backed up to the wall.

"Answer up, Meskin. Who are ye?"

"*Me llamo Chaco Cardenas y vivo en San Pedro en la estada de Tejas, señor.*"

"Shet up thet fast rattlin' and say it in plain English or I'll bust yer hide."

"I am Chaco Cardenas from San Pedro, Texas, sir."

"Thet's better, boy. Now, what're ye doin' up here, Meskin?"

Well, I could see why Mr. Story told us to be careful in this wild town. Just then, Mr. Story stepped into the saloon and we went with him.

"Hold on there, Morton! Mr. Cardenas is with us," Mr. Story said.

"So, we meet agin so soon, eh? Jist who're ye to keep buttin' in my business?"

"Nobody you care to know. Just leave us be and you won't git hurt none."

"You? Hurt me? I'll smash ye like a fly." He charged like a ragin' bull.

Mr. Story just waited 'til the last second and sidestepped

as Morton went crashing by. Story's rifle butt hit him on the side of his head and down he went.

"That head'll hurt fer a while. Let's mosey back to camp. Come on, boys, before he wakes up. Anybody tries to stop us gets what Morton got," Story said.

We went to our horses, and Chaco joined us, relieved to be alive and out of danger.

He spoke in good English, "Sirs, I'm grateful to you and wish to repay you."

"Come on to camp with us and let's see what's goin' on with yuh, Mr. Cardenas."

Well, me and Toby and Tab found us a new friend that day. Chaco was from a wealthy family south of San Antonio, Texas. They owned about twenty thousand acres of ranchland, and some crooked men were trying to take over the land. Chaco had been to Washington to get help in clearing the title to the land that Texas officials had been cold to respond to. They were too mad at Mexico to help any Mexican do anything except die.

That did not sound good to me because I wanted to go to Texas some day and be a ranger. Chaco was twenty-one and was taller than most Mexicans. Not many stood six-foot-one inches tall or weighed 175 pounds, except those who overloaded on beer and tequila all their lives.

"What's takeela?" Toby asked.

"It's like the white lightnin' Mr. Benton talks about. Whiskey," Tab said. "Sho nuff powerful stuff."

Chaco's mare was a deep red sorrel. Her coat was shined like it had oil on it. It showed signs of having excellent care.

"We raise these ourselves. We have over two hundred mares like this and a dozen stallions to match. I'll see to it that each of you get a horse or mare of your choice for the help you gave me."

"What's a mare?" Tab asked. "I thought it was a horse."

"It is, Mr. Tab. The male is called a horse, or *caballo*, and the female is a mare, or *yegua*. Come to my ranch and I'll give you one."

Well, right then and there we made a pact to come to Texas to see Chaco and his ranch.

The trip back home was great because Chaco agreed to come with us and stay a couple of days. He said the name of the ranch was *Rancho de Viboro*, which translated to Rattlesnake Ranch. It sure sounded spooky to me, but I meant serious business about going to Texas. My eyes lit up all the way home just thinking about Texas.

Chapter 5

Two days after Chaco left for Texas I got up early and headed for Julie's house because I wanted her to have the bear rug. Toby left for the Caddo settlement and took the smaller cub skin and a quarter of meat to the little girl who was hurt by the she-bear.

Julie saw me coming and ran out to see what I had. I jumped off my horse and took her hand. Before I knew what happened, she pulled me aside and behind a large bush and kissed me. I was surprised near out of my skin, but I kissed her back.

"Boy, sure is good to see you again."

"Me too, Jeff. What's that behind your saddle?"

I untied it and showed her the bearskin rug.

"Tab told me you had something, but I guessed it was store bought. I never thought of a rug you made. This is real special."

With that remark she hugged me again, and we kissed long and hard. I'll tell you right now, I was getting excited. Then Tab came and told us Mr. Benton was coming, so we made out to fix the bearskin rug so as to look like nothing was going on.

"Good day, Jeff. Looks like you had a good hunt."

"Yes, sir. We had a great time. Did Tab tell you about our trip?"

"Sure did, and I'm rightly proud of all of you."

"Well, it was surely excitin'. 'Specially when we had to get Tab and Chaco away from that terrible Mr. Morton. He frightens me."

"Oh, Jeff, I'm so proud of you," Julie said. "I could just hug your neck."

And she did and got away with it too. Even in front of her dad. I was rightly embarrassed, but he didn't say nothing except for me to stay for dinner, which I did. I wanted to go swimming with Julie that afternoon, but we didn't want her ma and pa to know. We had before and enjoyed it too and always was looking for times to go again.

Miz Benton and Julie and Tab's ma sure fixed a good meal. I didn't want them to think I didn't like it, so I ate seconds on near all of it. I didn't eat thirds because I didn't want to drown, so I politely lied and said I was full. Well, it was really true, so I didn't lie after all.

Miz Benton asked about Toby. I told her he had gone to the Caddo village to take a bearskin rug to the injured girl. Her Indian name was Morning Glory That Shines. They called her Glory for short. She was a small thing but was Toby's age. Anyway, they would enjoy the bear meat and she would have a good skin rug like Julie did.

"You boys are right nice to do this for the girls," she said. "Even if one of 'em is a heathen."

"Now, Mom," Mr. Benton said, "that ain't no way to speak about Toby's friend. After all, she ain't had no chance to learn Christianity like Julie, but maybe she will if we can help them some."

"I guess so," she replied. "But looks as how Toby would find a good white girl."

"Who and where?" Julie asked. "You know I'm the only one for miles around. Toby never did have somebody his age to play with at school except that Dawson girl, and she married last year when she turned fourteen."

"I forgot to tell you, Toby is goin' to Colorado with Mr. Story next month. He wants to make one more trip to a rondevoo with a couple of men he met in Cerro Gordo the other day. He said he'd take me and Toby, but I want to go to Texas and work for Chaco. Dad agreed to go with Toby and Mr. Story."

"Mr. Travers' cousin is here and wants to stay awhile, so he'll live at our place 'til Dad and Toby return."

"Oh, Jeff! How can you leave when I've got so much for us to do this summer?"

"Well, now. I'll jist be gone a few months, then I'll be back. Don't you fret none. Tab'll look after you."

"When you leavin', son?" Mr. Benton asked.

"Next Monday if Mr. Travers has my pistol fixed. I found it in the cave where we got the bears. He said he could put a new stock in it fer me. He said it looks like a French muzzle-loader flint lock with a powder funnel and a ramrod on it. I want to take it with me."

"Jeff, let's go walking. We only have a few days and you'll be gone. Come on. I know where some wildflowers are growing. We can pick some."

Well, I didn't have much choice except tell the Bentons thanks fer the meal and I'd see them 'fore I left fer Texas.

Me and Julie walked toward their big pond. I knew the place 'cause we played there many times. When we got there, Julie took my hands and looked at me with big tears in her eyes.

"You don't like me anymore or you'd stay here."

"Aw, Julie. Sure I like you. I jist want to go to Texas, but like I said, I'll come back. Promise."

Well, I'll tell you, we sure hated to part company that day. We just lay there in the shade and hugged and kissed for about two hours. She even told me I could have her if I wanted to. It wasn't that I didn't want to, but her being a preacher's daughter an' all, it just wasn't right. She agreed and we would wait, but it was hard to do.

I had that funny feeling in my stomach again, like when Ma died. I kept gettin' it every time I was with Julie. I guess I'd have to ask Pa about it sometime.

When I got home, Toby was back and he gave me something I was really proud of. Glory's mom had made two complete suits of buckskin, complete with leggin's and boots, one fer me and one fer Toby. His was a little too big, but he would grow to it. Mine was just right, and that night Toby gave me a new nickname I'd carry to my grave ... Buckskin Bradley. So, I guess we made a good trade.

"Sure suits me fine," I said. Toby and Dad echoed them too.

Chapter 6

Morton's head was hurting ten days later. He was rubbing it as he said to his two men, Jigger and Tomlin, "I'll get me that nigger Tab and that wild mountain man, what's his name?"

"Bill Story," Tomlin said.

"Yeah," Jigger echoed.

"Let's pack down to Willow Springs and find 'em. Maybe that Meskin is with 'em. I'd like to stick a knife between his ribs. That Tab is one fine nigger. Ought to fetch a fine piece of gold, say one thousand dollars. Might even sell him to the same man who bought his paw."

They packed provisions for several days and prepared the team and wagon for the trip to Willow Springs. The road was much longer than the trail. Jigger was astride a big gray gelding as Tomlin rode the wagon with Morton. Morton had designed the wagon himself. It had high sideboards and was covered with tanned hides so that any slaves inside could not be seen. Shackles were bolted to larger rings, which were fastened to the wood floor.

"Here's what we'll do, boys. We'll go by the Taafe place on the pretense of tradin' or buyin' some slaves and ask about others who might be interested in buyin' or sellin'."

The next day they approached the Taafe place and were met by George Taafe, two of his sons, and a host of dogs.

"Git down and rest a spell, folks. Goin' to be a hot one today."

"Howdy do, neighbor. The name's Morton, and this here handsome feller on the Gray is Jigger and this 'un is Tomlin. We shore appreciate the invite," Morton said as all were stepping to the ground. "We're on a mission of mercy to provide some poor souls with labor for their fields."

Taafe gave him a puzzled look, and Morton continued, "Jist a-lookin' fer some fine specimen of black flesh to provide work an' pleasure to those a needin' it. Heared they was a couple of good niggers over this way an' stopped in to see."

Taafe had heard of Morton and his bullish ways and wanted no dealings with him but invited them to eat and drink.

"We come down from Paraclifta through Anderson's Ferry. We're goin' on to Cook's Landin'," Morton lied. "Then we're goin' on east to Shoals and trade over that-a-way. Hope to pick up a load of black meat along the way."

"Don't have any fitten' to sell now," replied one of the sons. "We sold too many last year and will be shorthanded come crop time. We need to pick up some ourselves. If ye come back this way, we might be willin' to buy a couple of light bronze bed wenches."

"I'll see what I kin find fer ye. Say, where's that farmin'

preacher around here? Heared he was fixin' to sell out," Morton said.

"Don't know no farmin' preacher. Heared about a hellfire an' brimstone one over to Ashdown. Maybe he's it."

"We thank ye, Taafe," Morton replied. "We'll be goin'. Obliged fer the vittles an' rest."

After they were out of hearing range, Morton said, "Let's go south a ways so they'll think we're headin' fer Cooks Landin', then we'll cut over to Ashdown. I aim to fetch that one thousand-dollar nigger."

Chapter 7

Bill Story, Dad, and Toby had been gone about a week. They had first traveled up to Cerro Gordo, and two of Mr. Story's friends joined them for the journey to Colorado. I didn't know when I would ever see them again since I would be heading for Texas as soon as Mr. Traver's cousin was ready to come live at our place, which should've been the next week. I wanted to see Julie one more time, so I saddled up and headed for their farm.

I was nearly there when a horse and buggy came speeding toward me. Mr. Benton was driving and he yelled at me and pulled the horse to a quick stop. The buggy near turned over.

"What's wrong?" I yelled.

"It's Tab! Some men came and beat him last night and kidnapped him. They also hit his mama and threatened Julie when she tried to rescue him. They was too big and had guns too."

"Is Julie all right? I'll kill anybody who hurts her."

"She's fine for now but shook up a lot and worried about Tab. Julie says the man who took Tab must be the slave trader. He said Tab was his because he owned Tab's pa one time and there was no such thing as a free nigger."

I asked Mr. Benton where they went, and he said south toward the Red River. I knew he couldn't foller them and leave his wife and Julie and the farm and preaching an' all, so I told him I'd go.

"I'll get ready and go after them. I can cut across from my place after I git my guns and bedroll and stuff. They probably are headed for Texas to sell Tab. I'll find 'em."

I told him to tell Julie I'd come back as soon as I got Tab, even if I had to foller 'em to China. Mr. Benton gave me forty dollars to help buy food fer me and my horse. I hated to take it, but I had only twenty-five that Dad gave me when he left, and I knew I might not find work until I got to Chaco's ranch.

Well, Chaco's place would have to wait awhile. Seems like I read about "putting first things first" in the Good Book, and right now, Tab was in first place.

The only places I knew to cross into Texas was the ferry that landed on the New Boston side or the crossing about ten days' ride west. When I had everything gathered I rode in to see Mr. Travers and told him of my plans. His wife fixed me a sack of food. I headed south for the ferry.

I was glad fer one thing: the weather was good, and I could see the wagon trail. I even had the telescope Pa gave me fer looking long distances. They had two more and didn't need it. I surely did.

I felt like I had everything I needed, except I'd rather have

Toby or Pa fer company. Traveling alone is nice fer thinking about Julie and Ma and Pa, and especially about Julie. I missed her already and tried to remember what she looked like. For some strange reason, I couldn't quite get her in focus. Sure hoped she never found out. I'd only been gone one day.

I made camp after dark. Camp wasn't much to brag about. I didn't build a fire to cook. Instead, I ate some cold bread and meat along with dried apples. The bedroll was two blankets. This way I could be up and gone in a hurry. I was careful to feed and water my horse and fixed a picket for him so he wouldn't wander away. I liked him close by.

The next day I was up and away before first light. I ate some more bread and dried apples. With a little luck I could cut the trail of Morton and his buggy today.

I sure hadn't figured what to do when I caught up. I couldn't just charge in and take Tab. One or both of us might git killed. Maybe I could sneak in at night. I'd just have to wait and see.

I felt comfortable in the buckskins. They were so soft and good to sleep and travel in. I guess I was lucky that Toby had befriended the Indian girl. I kept lookin' fer buggy tracks as I approached the river and ferry. The fresh buggy tracks leading down to the ferry were wide and deep as if it was loaded with lumber and pulled by a team of mules.

"Howdy, son. Git down and visit a spell." The ferry owner smiled as I rode in.

"Good day, sir. Kin I git across tonight?"

"Nope. Takes too long and it's dark and dangerous. Stay the night and I'll have you across at daylight."

"In that case, I'll stay. Been riding two days and am tired and hungry."

"Where ye from, pilgrim? Ain't seen ye around these parts afore."

"Willow Springs, and I ain't never been down here before."

I saw a small hand printed sign that read:

FERRY
DRIFTY THOMAS, PROP.
10 CENTS

"Are you Mr. Thomas?"

"Sure am, son, and who might be askin'?"

"I'm Buckskin Bradley," I said sheepishly. It was the first time I had used the name outside of around Toby and Tab. It sounded purty good too.

"Buckskin Bradley, huh? Be ye named after the horse or clothes?"

"After my clothes, I reck'n. But I favor the buckskin horse 'cause he was a gift from my pa."

"Be yer pa Tom Bradley?"

I was surprised he knew my pa, but was glad fer the time to visit with someone who knew him.

"Yes, sir. He's my pa," I replied.

"Right sorry to hear about yer ma, son. She was a mighty good woman. Knew her folks back in Tennessee in Renfro Valley."

I had never seen Ma's folks but had heard her and Pa talk about them a-plenty. Toby and me even talked about goin' there sometime.

"What brung ye down here, son?"

"I'm tryin to find a man called Slave Trader Morton. He stole a free nigger named Tab from the preacher over at Ashdown."

"What's he to you, son? After all, he's jist another nigger."

Well, that riled me some. I hated to hear folks talk that way. So I said, "Right, jist like you are another whitey. He has feelin's and needs jist like us. Besides, he belongs to a man who treats him decent and his ma. I'm promised to the preacher's daughter."

"Yore shore right, son. I'se jist testin' yer grits. Shore proud ye feel that way. Heard tale of a preacher in Kaintuck name of Campbell who feels that way. Set a lot in store by him."

"Yes, sir, Mr. Thomas. This Campbell preaches the same as Mr. Benton. It's his man Tab I'm trailin."

"Well, son, yore shore on his trail, I reck'n. They came in here last night and made me haul 'em over in the dark. Didn't pay me, neither. Forced me at gunpoint too. Don't rightly like that 't'all."

I could tell Mr. Thomas was angry, so I asked him which way he thought they'd go.

"Heared one call the other Jigger, so reck'n one must be Morton. Mean-lookin' feller and loud talker, long handlebar mustache."

"That's them. Seen 'em once at Cerro Gordo. They tried to claim Tab then. Musta upset them when Mr. Story and some other men kept them from it."

"Somebody told me about that too. Say, didn't yore pa and Bill Story head up to Colorado? I hear lots on this river."

"They left last week and my little brother, Toby."

"Well, back to Morton. They said sumpin' bout San Antone. If it be where they be goin', foller this road southwest to the Sulfur River. Ye kin cross it on horseback easy enough and go on that way."

"Does this road lead to Austin? I surely would like to meet up with a Texas Ranger. Got a hankerin' to be one."

"Yep, jist go fer enough. Sure tough men, them rangers.

They's a Rangin' Company down south of here and maybe over to Jefferson somewheres. Seen one of 'em in Texarkana one time. Had two prisoners and headin' to Fort Worth to try 'em fer murder.

"Be sure and not ride that Buckskin too hard. He needs good care to go that long way. Ye kin ketch 'em in three or four days of steady ridin'. Probably don't 'spect no follerin'."

Chapter 8

Rain had been falling most of three days since I had left the Red River. There were no tracks to foller, but there was plenty of mud. Some of it so black and sticky, and my horse had a hard time pickin' up his feet.

I was lucky though. The Sulfur River did not rise much, so we crossed it without trouble. About the middle of the day, the sun broke through and it got hot and steamy. I came upon a small lake and decided to take a swim and cool off and rest my horse and maybe catch a fish or two.

The water felt good, and I was enjoyin' my swim when I looked up and saw two men on horseback near my horse that was tied to a tree. They looked to me like buffalo hunters or some type lowlife I'd heard about.

"Jist keep swimmin', son, and ye won't git kilt. We aim to take yore belongin's. We need 'em," said the bigger man.

He was a scraggly man with a rough beard and beady eyes

and about forty or so, I really couldn't tell. He musta weighed over 275 pounds. He had a gun pointed at me and there I was naked in the water. The smaller man was younger by some years. He got off his horse and started huntin' through my stuff.

"Looky here, Brace. I found his pot of gold," he said.

Luckily, he had found only the twenty-five dollars I had in my buckskins. The other forty dollars that Mr. Benton gave me was hidden in a secret place in my saddle.

"Good," Brace said. "Come on, let's git. We'll leave your horse down the road a piece. Don't ye foller us, kid, or you'll regret it."

They left and led my horse away. They didn't even take my clothes. I guess they weren't afraid of me. They even left my pistol after throwin' the shells in the lake. I guess all they wanted was my money.

I dressed and started after them. It took me near an hour to git to the place where they left my horse. My rifle was missing and so was the telescope. However, their tracks were plain as day in the mud and they was goin' southwest, so I went after them. It was still two hours 'til sunset, and I looked carefully ahead so I wouldn't stumble upon them. I wanted to sneak up on them.

They musta thought I wouldn't have nerve enough to foller them because they was real noisy and braggin' about the money they took offen me. That made it easy fer me to git close enough to hear 'em.

I had found a long stick that I sharpened to a spear point. In a few minutes, one of the men walked to the edge of the clearin' to relieve himself. He came within three steps of where I was hid. With his pants down, he was an easy target fer me. I eased the spear point right up between his legs from behind and whispered to him, "Don't make a sound or this spear will go all the way up yore innards."

He looked up in surprise but didn't move. I got his pistol from the pocket and also the money he had taken. So far, so good. I went to his horse and got a rope and also a bandana from a saddle bag. I went behind a big tree and tied him and put the bandana around his mouth for a gag.

Brace musta thought he was takin' a long time and hollered out to 'im.

"What's takin' so long? I'm hungry."

I didn't say anything, jist started walkin' toward 'im with my head covered so he wouldn't know it wasn't his pardner. I got near enough and pulled the pistol and aimed it at Brace. As big as he was and as close, it would be hard to miss. He looked in surprise and raised his hands.

"Where'd ye come from, boy, and where's Whitey? Careful with that gun."

"Guess you know where I come from and why I came. Whitey, if he's yore pardner, is tied and gagged back there. The three of us are goin' to Jefferson to the sheriff. Mount up and let's git goin'."

I tied his hands behind his back and helped both on their horses. It took us about an hour to get to Jefferson, and we found that the sheriff's office was clear to Daingerfield. I didn't even know where that was and didn't want to go at night. I took them to the stable and made a deal with the hostler to bed them down 'til daylight. At least they'd be tied and could sleep under their own blankets.

Sometime during the night I woke up and started to git up when somethin' pounded me on the head. I came to my senses about daylight and had no clothes on. All my gear was gone. So was my horse, saddle, gun, money, and everything.

The hostler was not around either. I was in a sad state of affairs.

I had been dreamin' about Mom and Dad and Toby back in Arkansas. I was missin' all of 'em terrible. They had been in my thoughts often the past few days. Sure wished Dad was there. He could've helped me catch that Morton.

About then a man and a young girl came in. I hid in one of the empty stalls. They had a blanket and some clothes. The man said, "Son, put these clothes on and come on out."

"How'd you know I was in here?"

"Milly, that there's my girl, she came in for our buggy and saw you laid out on the floor."

I got that feelin' in my stomach agin jist thinkin' about her seein' me without any clothes on. I couldn't even look at her. After I told them what happened, they said I could come with them to their place fer a few days 'til I recovered. The knot on my head needed to be seen by the doctor to prevent infection since it was bleeding kinda bad. The man's name was Tom Morgan, and he had a small ranch west of town. I was embarrassed but was glad to go. Strange way to git welcomed to a strange town.

The head required seven stitches, and Mr. Morgan paid fer it. That was some more money I owed and couldn't pay fer now. I'd have to work it off if they'd let me. The buggy ride to their place pounded my head somethin' terrible, but I never let on. We got to the barn and I helped put the horse and buggy up. Then we went in the house. It was a big place compared to ours in Arkansas. It had a big room in front, another room next to it was a bedroom, with another smaller bedroom off to the west. Behind the big bedroom was a kitchen with a pantry full of lots of canned peaches and the like.

Mr. Morgan took me back to the barn and showed me

the tack room. It was like a leather factory with several harnesses, saddles, bridles, and all kinds of ropes. Only they called 'em lariats. Came from the Mexicans' word *reata,* they said. Behind the tack room was a feed room with grain sacks and some feed bundles. I knew what those were since I had grown up stackin' 'em on our farm. Another room was next to the feed room. It had two bunks in it. One was on top of the other.

"This is yore room. You can stay here as long as you need to. We eat at dawn every mornin'. If ye ain't ailin', don't be late or ye'll miss a meal."

"I shore am thankin' ye, Mr. Morgan. I'll be on time. Also, I'll help pay my keep by workin' at whatever ye need done."

"Jist take it easy fer a couple of days, Jeff. There's plenty of time to work when ye git well enough."

"Most folks know me by Buck, which is short fer Buckskin." Then I told him about Toby and the Indians and how I got the name of Buckskin.

"Buck it is, then. I'll tell Milly when we git in the house. Might as well come on in. She'll have a bite fer us to eat by now."

Chapter 9

I was still havin' a hard time lookin' at Millie. I had been workin' at their place a month, and we hadn't said five words to each other. I got along fine with Mr. Morgan. He worked right alongside me all day. I told him about losin' Ma and about Dad, Toby, and Mr. Story. I also told him about wantin' to find Tab.

"Saw them a day or so before we found you. Big feller, handlebar mustache and all. Said they was goin' to San Antone."

"That's where I want to go when I git you paid off. Tab is my friend, and he is a free man and his ma and the preacher man want him back. They raised him."

"Tell you what, son. You work fer me for two more weeks and we'll both go. I want to take my family down near Austin to visit my wife's brother. We'll all go by wagon and horseback. Beck, her brother, has some fine yearlings to sell me and we can drive them back here."

"Sure would appreciate it, Mr. Morgan. I'll go."

"Reck'n you'll have to go all the way to Clarksville to find a sheriff. Ain't none here or in Daingerfield or Boston. Might as well fergit it or try to find the thieves yoreself. We might run acrost 'em if we ask around and keep our eyes an' ears open."

"Thanks, Mr. Morgan. We'll do jist that."

★

We decided to travel overland to Austin, since the travel by boat or barge would take us to New Orleans, which was a long way from Austin. If we chose, we could drive the cattle to Indianola and ship them to New Orleans and up the Red River to Clarksville and then down to Jefferson. We could decide that later.

The wagon was loaded with our provisions. I chose to ride a horse provided by Mr. Morgan since he would be riding one too. Milly and her mother would take turns driving the wagon. Roddy, her younger brother, would ride in the wagon. He was eight. He could ride a horse or drive the wagon. He also was a pretty good shot with a rifle. We headed south to Nacogdoches and would then go southwest to Austin.

After about two days we came to the Sabine River. There was my horse stolen from me by the men a few months before. It had the saddle on it and also my rifle was slid into a kind of boot holding it. The men were about one hundred yards downriver fishing. I tied the horse behind the wagon, and we drove it to where the men were fishing and drinkin'. They didn't notice us 'til I spoke up.

"Howdy, friends. Be obliged if you would raise yore hands and listen up a spell."

"What the—"

"I said listen up. This here rifle aimed at your gut means business. You left me fer dead, stole all my belongings, which I now have back. All I need is the buckskins offen that man over there and sixty-five dollars taken from me and the saddle."

"Ain't never seen ye, son. Couldn't have been us."

"You answer to Brace and we want what's ours. Otherwise, we gut shoot you and ride on. Who wants to be first? You, you little pipsqueak, or the big, fat boss man?"

"Hold on there, boy. We didn't mean ye no harm. Jist needed some fixin's. Ye jist happened to be there."

"We're here now, so shuck my buckskins and give us the money," I said.

"Not in front of the women, we won't."

Mr. Morgan said, "This rifle says you do, so do it." He aimed the rifle at the man wearing my buckskins. He did. All the money they had added up to fifty-seven dollars, which we took.

"We'll collect the rest if we ever see you again," Morgan said.

The women watched and seemed really amused. I was embarrassed knowin' that Milly was seein' a naked man again, but she jist grinned at 'em. We gathered the things, put them in the wagon, and crossed the Sabine. All the time I kept my eyes on them, darin' 'em to foller us. They didn't. I was lucky to git my things back, even the pistol I had found at Pauley's Cave. I explained it to Milly at suppertime around the campfire. I left out the part about a certain girl back at Willow Springs. I felt funny since I had barely thought about her for several days. Wonder why?

Chapter 10

We made camp on the river east of town. I wanted to git up early and see if I could find a Texas Ranger. I stopped a man on the edge of town. He was a local man and gave me directions to the ranger's office. There was one man in the office.

"Come in, son. What be yer problem?"

"My name is Jeff Bradley, but my friends call me Buckskin or Buck. I want to be a Texas Ranger."

"Well, my name is Burl Maxey, and I'm a Texas Ranger. Have been fer quite a spell. Why ye wantin to be one?"

"Met one a few years back and he impressed me. I like law and order and wanted to see if ye needed any new blood."

"We always need more men. Lots of territory in Texas needin' coverin. How old be ye?"

"Eighteen."

"Rekin thet's old enough. Where ye from and what do ye folks say about it?"

"I'm from Willow Springs up in Arkansas and ain't got a ma no more. She died last year. Pa took my brother, Toby, and went with some fellers to the west somewheres to rondevoo with some mountain men. Pa knows I want to be a ranger."

"We need to check yer background some. Who is the law where ye lived?"

He grilled me fer about another hour and finally remarked, "We need a man southwest of here around San Antone. Lost one last week in a war there. Some fellers tryin to take over a big ranch owned by some Meskins. Kin you shoot a rifle and pistol?"

"Sure can and purty good too. I can outshoot my pa any day. Don't know about shootin' a man, but I ain't afeard of any of 'em."

I told him about my run-in with Slave Trader Morton and the men who stole my belongin's and me gittin' 'em back. I also told about knowin' the Cardenas son whose ranch he was tellin' about and about wantin' to go see him. I wanted to tell about Tab and wantin' to find him, but it added up to a lot of wantin', so I held back on that.

"Tell you what, Buck. Ye stay put fer a few days. I'll do some checkin' and will ride out to see ye about three or four days. We might work out a trade."

I rode back to camp and told the folks about my possible job as a ranger. They was proud fer me, but I detected a little disappointment in the voice of a certain girl. I guess I was about to foul up another friendship. I made myself useful around camp by haulin' water and choppin' wood. Seems we always needed more wood. I was glad to keep busy.

Ranger Maxey came on Tuesday. Me and Milly was haulin' water. We stopped and greeted him, and I introduced him to Milly. Her Dad walked up, so I introduced him to Mr. Morgan.

"Buck, I reck'n we need to talk. Ye kin sit in, Mr. Morgan." We went to the campfire area, and Milly joined her mom and busied themselves with fixin' supper.

About an hour later, we said our good-byes to Ranger Maxey. I could barely believe what had taken place. Before he left, I was sworn in as a new deputy Texas Ranger, given a badge, ten dollars fer some shells fer my gun that came off the dead ranger. He also gave me the belt and holster that went with it.

Mr. Morgan filled me in on the details of the trade fer the cattle from his kin. We would drive them to Indianola and ship them by barge to Jefferson. After that, I could go on the Cardenas Ranch. Burl Maxey wanted me to go to the ranch and git a job there. He didn't want me wearin' the badge but to work undercover and try to find the man who killed Ranger Poe. Wc planned to drive the cattle starting tomorrow.

★

The trip was without problems. Only one cow died, and that was from a snakebite. We penned the cattle in the yards at the boat docks and went to eat. The barge would not leave for three days, and Mr. Morgan didn't need me, so I left early the next morning. Milly hugged me farewell, and I was surprised the funny feelin' in my stomach wasn't there. I told the Morgans good-bye, and he paid me fifty dollars for the work I had done. I promised to come see them sometime and headed west.

About an hour later, I came upon a train of wagons loaded with bales of cotton headed fer the barges, apparently bound fer New Orleans or some distant place. I nodded my head in greeting to the man on horseback in front of the first wagon. As I passed the wagons, one of the black men driving the team looked me over carefully. So did the man on the next wagon. They looked a lot alike, like a father and son, or maybe older and younger brothers.

I rode on but couldn't shake the hauntin' feeling that I knew one of the men. It struck me then. That was Tab and probably his pa. They hadn't recognized me or didn't let on if they did. I turned and slowly followed them back to Indianola. I was formulating a plan as I rode. The wagons stopped fer a meal, so I rode wide around them so I would not be seen. I went straight to the Morgans' camp and told Mr. Morgan of my plan. He agreed to help. So did Milly.

We watched as the wagons were unloaded at the docks. The man who rode in front of the wagons gathered the drivers and put them all in one wagon. They had shackle and chains on one leg. He then chained them together so one couldn't run away. Mr. Morgan, Milly, and I started to execute the plan.

I put my ranger badge on and walked over to the man.

"I'm Ranger Bradley. I need to talk to you. What's yer name, Mister?"

"The name's Watson, what's it to you?"

"You have two men there who violated this girl here up at Jefferson. I'm here to take 'em back fer hangin'."

I saw Tab look at me and knew he was aware of who I was. He poked the man next to 'im. It musta been his pa. Neither said anything.

Watson spoke angrily, "Well, if you want 'em, ye'll have to pay me two thousand dollars, which is what I paid fer 'em."

"We don't pay to take prisoners. Who did ye buy 'em from?"

"None of yer business. Now git and leave us alone."

"I'm makin it my business," I said as I pulled out my pistol and pointed it at Watson. "Now, who did you steal or buy these men from?"

He saw how serious I was and replied, "Slave Trader Morton."

"Him again. I guess you greedy folks will never learn. He never bought a slave in his life worth anything. Most of 'em, he stole. Like these two."

I pointed my finger at Tab and his Pa. Their eyes lit up, but they remained silent.

"Unlock the shackles on them. They belong to me. You settle up with Slave Trader Morton."

I looked at Tab and his Pa and asked, "Did you two ever belong to Slave Trader Morton?"

"No, suh," Tab said. His pa said the same.

"See, Watson. These two are coming with me. Unlock 'em, now."

He did.

I took Tab and his pa away from there as fast as they could walk. When we got back to the Morgan camp, I got down and grabbed Tab and shook his hand and gave him a big hug.

"Mr. Jeff," he cried, "I couldn't believe it was really you. I told Pa as soon as I seen you, but we didn't let on. I was hopin' you'd know it was me."

"I didn't know at first, but when I saw the man behind you in the next wagon, you favored so much. I realized it had to be you. I made a plan and got Mr. Morgan and Milly here to help me."

Tab and his pa thanked us again, then we told them the rest of the plan. Tab's pa was to go with the Morgans to Jefferson and deliver the cattle. Tab could go if he wanted to, but I wanted him to come with me to work on the Cardenas

Ranch. Yes, he remembered the Çardenas name from the time in Cerro Gordo and his visit to our house. Tab wanted to come with me.

I went alone into town and bought a horse and gear for Tab. His pa would get the same when they arrived in Jefferson. We said good-bye to the Morgans, and Tab and I both had tears in our eyes as we told his pa good-bye. His pa promised to tell a certain pretty girl hello fer me and that I was doin' fine.

Chapter 11

It took all morning fer me to tell Tab about my trip to find him. I didn't leave out anything. He was proud of the way I recovered my belongings from the men who stole them. Then he told me of the journey to the farm where his pa was. The trade by Slave Trader Morton was done and Tab was reunited with his pa. I fergot to tell that Tab's pa was named Moses. They had planned on trying to escape when the cotton was delivered to Indianola. Guess we made that possible fer them.

Our ride from Indianola to near San Antone would take several days, but we had plenty of supplies furnished by the Morgans. Our horses were fresh from a day's rest, so we slowly made our way west. Tab had never been more jovial.

"Buck, I reck'n I'll ferever be in yore debt fer what ye done fer us."

"I was glad it worked out this way. Yore my best friend, and friends were meant to do good things fer each other."

"Shore would like to see Ma and also yore little brother, Toby. Tell me where they was goin'."

I spent the next hour talking about Pa, Toby, and Mr. Story and what they had told me about their planned trip to the mountains. About three days later we were camped about fifty miles southeast of Austin on the Colorado River.

Tab asked, "Why does the river have that name way down here in Texas?"

"Don't rightly know, Tab. Guess it jist does."

We heard sounds of gunfire in the distance. I'd never been around a war, but this sure sounded like it might be one. We broke camp and headed upriver to see what it was. A group of uniformed men were coming our way, so we got behind some heavy brush and trees and listened as they went by. One of the men was braggin' about how many redskins he'd killed. Another said he'd got more'n that.

I couldn't tell what kind of army they were from their uniforms, but they were not Mexican. I guessed they must've been American or Texican army. We got back on the trail up the river and shortly came upon a terrible scene. There were hundreds of Indian bodies lying around the area. Many of them were old men, old women, and children. We didn't see many men of fighting age among the dead. It was a bad day fer us.

"Let's go on to Austin and notify somebody. Maybe someone will know what to do."

We rode upriver and about an hour later, we came upon a camp of Indians. Slowly, with hands up in greeting, we rode to their camp. They invited us down.

When I spoke to the men, one answered in good English. That surprised us both.

"We jist come from a camp about one hour from here on the river. Several hundred people were murdered," I said. We were asked to tell what all we saw. Their faces were grim, and it musta been hard to hold back the tears.

We told them we would go into Austin and notify the authorities. They thanked us and we left, not knowing anything else we could do. The ride into Austin took the rest of the day, so we camped at the edge of town so we could go in early the next morning.

We found the sheriff's office and told him who we were and what we had seen the day before.

"Sounds like the Cabbott Army to me. They are a renegade outfit of about a hunderd men or so. Only I don't like to call 'em men. They's mostly cowards who shoot from behind or in the dark. You two had better be careful. They only attack Indians, Blacks, and Mexicans. I'll round up some men and investigate. Likely they headed southeast into the brush country around Gonzales."

I told the sheriff again about the camp of Indian men so he would be aware of them. He asked us, "Where are you going?"

"We're going to visit and perhaps work for the Cardenas Ranch. I think it is near Frio Town," I said.

"Yore right about that. It is between the Hondo and Frio Rivers. Good ranch and good people too. They're in a war there with some folks tryin' to steal their ranch from 'em. Not much I can do fer 'em. Too far away from here. Hope you might be of help. They could use it. Good luck to you both."

"Thanks, Sheriff. Hope we can meet again sometime."

Tab expressed his thanks as well, and we rode southwest.

The first sign of light the next morning, a young Indian boy about sixteen or seventeen years old rode into camp. He was well-built and had a shorter haircut than most young Indians I had seen. He rode straight up in the saddle. His horse was a good-looking Overo about fifteen hands high and well-muscled. It had been well taken care of. He greeted us with, "I need to talk with you men. I came from the camp where the slaughter took place and understand you were there first."

"We sure hated the sights we saw. Couldn't help in any way we knew about except to report to the authorities in Austin."

He said his name was Tall Toad but went by the name of Toady. We gave him our names and told him where we were going. He wanted to go with us, since his mother, sister, and younger brother had been killed on the river. His father had died when he was a small boy. We gladly let him join us.

Toady had a fine horse, a saddle that needed repair, an old rifle that didn't work, a good hand-made knife with a seven-inch blade, sharpened on both sides. He also had a good water bag. With a little help from me and Tab, Toady was fixed up and ready to travel. So was I. We had bought Tab a set of clothes and a hat, some new boots, and a raincoat. We were fit to travel to San Antone. As we leisurely rode west, we all three shared some of our past with each other. Seemed to me, the three of us made a good team, kinda like them Three Musketeers we read about in school. I had to explain that to Tab and Toady.

We talked about how best to approach the rancho, as we referred to it. It was decided that I would go to the ranch first, then after a couple of days, Tab and Toady would arrive, looking for a job of some kind. Tab was a good cook, so he might get on in that job. Toady proved to be good with horses even at his young age.

When we got within about two miles of the ranch, according to directions given us by a man in the last town we came through, we heard rifle shots somewhere in front of us. We carefully approached, and I gradually worked my way closer as Tab and Toady slowed their pace to allow distance between us. We did not want anyone to see us together.

When I topped a slight rise, I saw two men on horseback running toward us at a fast clip. I moved to the side of the road into a clump of scrub oak and shinnery. The men slowed their horses and finally came to a complete stop. I could hear them as they spoke.

"Naw, I don't think he saw us, but don't know where he went. Maybe into that bunch of brush."

I was amazed at the clearness of their voices. Sound apparently carried well in this country. As they came closer, I slowly moved away from the direction they were coming, being careful to hold my hand on the muzzle of my horse to prevent any sound coming from him and hoping their horses didn't make any sounds to alarm them of my presence. Maybe the heavy breathing caused by their recent run prevented them from any problem.

Finally, they had gone all the way through the clump of trees and were satisfied that I had disappeared. They returned the way they had come in, so I made my way slowly back to the road, hoping Tab and Toady had found some cover. I would soon find out if shots were heard. When I got to the road I looked both ways and saw no one but two sets of tracks leading back the way I was coming when I turned off the road. I made my way toward the ranch.

As I neared the gate area of the ranch, I was met by a rider with a rifle. He ordered me to stop and identify myself. I was sure hoping Chaco had told them about me and they would recognize my name.

"Señor, my name is Jeff Bradley, and I am a friend of Chaco. He stopped by in Arkansas and stayed a few days with me."

"Chaco will decide if you are his friend. Carefully hand your gun to me and don't make any fast moves."

I was surprised at his well-spoken English but did as he suggested. He ordered me to proceed in front of him as we made our way about half a mile to the ranch headquarters. As we neared the building, we were met by a group of riders, all well-armed. They took the reigns of my horse and led me to the main building. As we got there, a tall, slender *vaquero* came off the porch and called out, "Señor Jeff. Welcome to my rancho. When I saw you coming, I told my sister to prepare some food and refreshment for you."

"Hello, Chaco, my friend. Shore glad to see you. I didn't know if I would be welcome after the two men met me on the road."

He had a questioning look on his face and asked me to explain. As we went inside, his sister, Rosita, met us with a smile that would stop a clock. She had the cooled drinks and a sandwich.

"Welcome, sir, and thank you for saving the life of my brother."

Apparently, Chaco had shared his experiences with her after he got home last year. Chaco introduced me to all the men who came into the room. One was his foreman, Luis, another his top hand, Renaldo, and two others whose names I couldn't pronounce, but one sounded something like Viloreal, only he said it like Viyoreal. I learned later that two letter L's together sounded like a Y. The other was named Ignacio, I think. Anyway, I was glad to get a good reception from all of them, especially from the beautiful Rosita. Her name I could remember.

"Chaco, I need to tell you of events that led me here."

"Please do, and if it is fine with you, Rosita would love to hear it as well."

"She may not like some of it, but I'll do my best not to embarrass her too much."

"That would be difficult, Señor Jeff. She was raised with four brothers and knows more than both of us about life."

At any rate, I did my best to tell of all the events surrounding the taking of Tab by the Slave Trader Morton, my run-in with the thugs that led me to Jefferson, and I left out the part about being left naked by the thugs and being found by a beautiful daughter of the man who nursed me back to health.

"Sounds like you been having a bad time, Señor Jeff, or do you want to be called Buck?"

"Either will do, my friend, but I like the Buck part better."

"Then Buck it will be, and I'll tell my family to call you Buck."

"One or two more things I want to tell you. Do you remember telling me you had been clear to Washington with your problem?"

"That is what brought me through your country, Buck. Why do you ask?"

"It is getting results, finally."

"I don't see any. How do you mean?"

"Yore lookin' at one. I am now a Texas Ranger sent here to help you."

"Then I am doubly proud to have you here."

"One request I have is to put me on as a regular ranch hand and keep my ranger job a secret. I talked it over with

Ranger Captain Burl Maxey in Austin, and he suggested we do it this way."

"Consider it done, friend Buck. You mentioned having another thing to share with me. What is it? I hope it is as good as the last one."

I looked over at Rosita, and she gave me a great big smile of approval at what I had shared with them. I was shore goin' to enjoy knowin' her.

"Do you remember meetin' Tab, the black boy we had with us at my farm?"

"Sure do. How is he?"

"He is fine now and glad to be with me again. He was stolen by Slave Trader Morton and his dad, Moses, was taken years ago by the same man. I was really lucky to run across them on the trip to help drive the cattle to Indianola, and we managed to get them both away from him."

"That must have been exciting, Señor Buck. You must tell me and Rosita about it sometime. Where is Señor Tab now?"

"He is somewhere near this ranch now. Let me explain."

So I told them about Tab and Tall Toad and our calling him "Toady" now. They would show up here soon looking for work. I told them that Tab would be a fine cook or ranch hand and Toady had a good way with horses. I asked them not to reveal that I was a friend or even knew them and that it may work out better in the long run for no one to know. I explained about the massacre Tab and I had come up on and later how Toady had found our camp. Since he was the only survivor, we took him in and were now traveling with him.

"All this is with the approval of our ranger captain, but he has no money to pay them for their help."

"Do not worry, Señor Buck. If we save this rancho, we will

all have plenty of *dinero* and will gladly hire them now for the work they do."

Chapter 12

Four days after Buck came to the Rattlesnake Ranch, Tab and Toady rode in. Buck and Chaco, along with five vaqueros, were working on a few cattle that needed dehorning. Four vaqueros rode up to the corral and brought an Indian and a black man, apparently a nigger or Negro. They were introduced to Chaco, who in turn introduced them to Buck Bradley. No secret eye movements or other signs revealed the truth between the three friends.

Chaco invited them to the bunk house along with Buck. After talking to them for a time, he told them to unsaddle their horses and pick a bunk. He wanted them to stay on at least for the summer. Both thanked Chaco and promised to give a good day's work for the twenty-five dollars and "found" they would be paid each month. They had never had such a good offer; neither did they expect this one. They were in "hog heaven" even on a cattle ranch. All of them would have to get used to the Mexican way of life as well as the language. Both were eager to try and learn.

A few days later, Chaco and his new men were invited to ride with him out on the range. As they rode he explained the job ahead of them, as well as the lay of the land as he pointed out the two rivers. The rancho was bordered on the west by the Leona and on the east by the Frio. Both had their headwaters far to the northwest of San Antone.

He told them the rancho was a gift of a large land grant given to several prominent families from Mexico by the *presidente* of Mexico. Chaco's grandfather was one of the recipients. The rancho was about 7,200 *hectares* in size, or about eighteen thousand acres. Since it was between two rivers, it was a choice location for a cattle ranch as well as good farmland. It was small in size compared to King Ranch, but Richard King was a wealthy shipbuilder who established his ranch some years before and started the Santa Gertrudis breed of cattle. This name came from a larger grant from Mexico years earlier. Chaco had managed to buy two bulls of that breed, but they refused to sell any heifers to anyone who was not a member of the King Family. The only way to get a heifer was to cross the bulls with various breed cows for several generations until a heifer showed enough Santa Gertrudis characteristics to be considered one. This was usually about seven-eighth pure by then.

The tour of the whole ranch would take several days, so they only saw a small part of it. They got a pretty fair picture of the place after Chaco told them all he intended.

"When you were accosted by the two men on the way here, Buck, they are a major part of my problem. It was either one or both brothers or their vaqueros, or, rather, henchmen. The brothers are from a German family near the little city of Fredericksburg. They are trying to run us off so they can take over this land."

"Is that town around here?" Buck asked.

"No, it is about as far north of Santone as we are south of it, which makes it around 125 to 150 miles and almost due north of us."

"How can they match forces with you if they are so far away?" Buck asked.

"There are a number of smaller German villages where they can hire men to do the dirty jobs they want done. That is probably what they are doing, and the local law enforcement people have some Germans among them and refuse to get involved. That is why I chose to go to Washington. The people in Austin have some German blood in their politics also.

"I'll keep explaining the problems as we see them in days to come. Just rest assured, this job of protecting my rancho will not be an easy one. I have about seventy-five vaqueros on the ranch, but very few have weapons or know how to use them except for a knife. We are all trained from our childhood to use those. Some are also good with a bow and arrows. Toady, can you help us there?"

"Yes, Señor Chaco. My father and brothers taught me well. I'll do what I can to pass it on to those who want it or need to learn it."

"Gracias to you. We will need all the help we can get," Chaco said. "Just get with Ignacio when we get back to the rancho headquarters, and he will help you with materials and men to learn."

I guess the next month or two went by without a hitch. At least we didn't hear of any problems, and we all worked every day at our jobs with our guns handy if needed. The work was very hard, dusty, and yet it was enjoyable. We liked the pace the Mexican vaqueros worked. They never seemed to get in a hurry but could hold the same pace for several hours. We had good meals twice and sometimes three times a day. Every night I went to bed tired and gradually got in better shape physically. Chaco said we would. A few times, Tab and I would whisper with each other and encourage one another. Tab would then tell Toady to keep up his work. He fit in real good.

One day Chaco told us to be ready tomorrow for some good fun. He had his drovers bring in a bunch of green colts that needed some training. We all tried our hand at riding some of them the next morning. Toady told us we were goin' about it all wrong. His grandfather had taught him a better way to break a horse that would not hurt him or the vaquero who was trying to be the boss. We each bet him that he could not break as many in a month as anyone else could. He was sure confident.

We each got to select five horses, put halters on them, and helped lead them to an area away from the rest. I found a grove of trees about a mile east that had a small creek near it. I built a little corral with some of the trees I cut and dug post holes and set them to erect a fence. I wondered what Tab and Toady and some of the vaqueros were doin', but I never asked. The work proved to be very tiring, painful, and downright exasperatin' at times, but I kept it up. About twenty-five or twenty-six days later, Chaco came to the bunk house and announced that the horses were to be brought back over the next two days. We were glad.

It had been agreed that each of us would put five dollars into a pot and the one who did the best job got all the money. It was a "winner take all" deal, and no side bets were allowed. Sure was a lot of wondering on that Saturday when we had to show what we had done with our selections. Chaco put some numbers in a hat, and each of us drew one, which gave the order for each one. I drew number seven, Tab number eight, and Toady number ten. The other vaqueros had the other seven numbers since there were ten of us competing with fifty horses.

It was agreed that we would begin in order from one to ten. After about a fifteen-minute interval, the order would be reversed and then reversed each time. This way every vaquero would have equal opportunity to show what he'd done with his five green horses. This procedure would take two days, but the ranch would have fifty more horses added to its string. Each vaquero could choose any two other vaqueros to help in saddling and bridling and even holding his horse.

The only other requirement was that a vaquero had to use his own saddle each time unless a cinch strap broke or it proved otherwise unuseful. Seemed fair to me.

The first rider was Juan Rodriquez, and his two chosen men helped catch a rather tall, sixteen-hands-high sorrel mare that was an eye-catcher. She bucked him off on the second jump and ran to the other side of the arena. Two of us hazed her back around so his helpers could catch her and he mounted again. This time, he lasted eight jumps. Since there was a twenty-minute time limit, time ran out before he could mount again. I was afraid to taunt him; I probably could do no better, maybe even worse.

Guillermo Villa was next. He rode his gelding, as did the next three riders. I was getting nervous, as my time was coming soon, but I did my best to encourage the riders as each mounted. Rider six was the nephew of the owner. He was Philipe, and he was a good horseman whose big gelding stood over sixteen and almost seventeen hands high. He also had a wide barrel, and one needed long legs to reach around him, but Philipe was about five foot eight inches and had no chance of that. He depended on riding skill, which he had plenty of. After three quick buck-offs, he was successful.

My first ride was on a chestnut mare about fifteen hands high. I got lucky and only lost my seat once before a successful ride. Tab was not so lucky and lost out after losing his seat four times as time ran out. We eagerly awaited Toady's ride. Tab and me helped him, but it was really not needed. When his gelding was led into the center of the ring, Toady asked everyone to move away to the fences. He did not even want his horse tied.

He picked up his bridle, blanket, and saddle and gradually walked out to him as he quietly spoke to the horse. He walked slowly around the gelding, and two or three times he slowly reached out and touched, then massaged him in the area where he touched him. Finally, he placed the blanket on his back, followed by the saddle. After cinching up, he removed the rope halter, put the bridle on, then just mounted the gelding and rode around the arena. We were amazed at what we saw. Then the cheers and whistles started. We had never seen anything like it.

When he stopped, we all gathered around to shake his hand and said, "If you can do that with one more horse, we are willing to concede." He wanted us to pick one of his remaining horses. Of course, we all picked the big stallion, which he agreed would be harder. We got it to the center of the arena and turned it completely loose, no halter, no rope, no nothing. We moved away, as he suggested, and he repeated the exact procedure as before. Absolutely amazing.

Chaco declared him the winner and surprised us by this remark, "Mañana, each of you will have the five horses you have selected. You may break them as you choose. I suggest you each pay Toady to break yours or at least teach you his secrets. He told me what he could do. I believe him now. Do you?"

We all answered, "Sí, yes, Señor. Absolutely." Then the questions started pouring in to Toady, which he said he would answer over the next few days and months. He did too. I was anxious to learn the new way. So were the rest of the crew. Looked to me like Toady had a job for life there if he wanted it. I sure hoped so.

The days stretched into weeks, then months, without much interference from the German families. Then one night before the month of November ended, there was a big hay fire at one of the camps, and two of Chaco's vaqueros were killed. Apparently, they were asleep when shots were fired and died before knowing what happened. The third camp worker escaped and reported the deaths.

Chaco asked me to ride with him to the site. There were tracks of five horses that led to the east from the camp, so we followed them for five miles. It was obvious that it was the same group that had been active before. They had rounded up some cattle and trailed them to the river, and their tracks were lost in the cattle tracks.

"We had about two thousand cows and steers at this camp, and I guess about two hundred to three hundred head are missing. Tomorrow, we will ride across the river and see where they went. First, we'll go back for more help and come prepared for war," he said.

"Were either of the vaqueros married?" I asked.

"No, but both have families that work for me. This will be hard on them."

We rode back to headquarters by dark.

Chaco related our findings, and twenty-five men volunteered to ride, so Chaco selected ten of them along with Tab, Toady, and me. That would make fourteen, and on the way we would swing north and pick up a brother of one of the dead men.

Chapter 13

The trail of the cattle went southeast from the river. After about a mile, the trail turned back to the south and a little west. Chaco drew us a map in the dirt that suggested a course east of Artesia Wells, which, if followed, would take us to Laredo and to Old Mexico. If we could not overtake them, the cattle would disappear in Mexico. Maybe luck was on our side since we could move much faster than the cattle. That's what we decided to do, so we set a faster pace.

I was riding a big sorrel gelding about sixteen hands high. He had plenty of "bottom" and was very gentle every morning and did not try to buck at any time. I had chosen well. Tab and, of course, Toady had good mounts under them too. Sure was grateful to Toady for teaching us to "gentle break" the horses.

Chaco laid out a plan for us that night. The next day at daybreak, he took Tab and five of his vaqueros and headed a little more southwest to try to get around the cattle before they got to Cotulla, about twenty miles ahead. The rest of us were to follow the cattle and get as close as possible without alerting the thieves. We were to meet at Cotulla if we did not overtake the herd. If we did catch them, I was to go around and let Chaco know where we were.

With all the oak and scrub oak along, with several variety of cacti, we were happy to have very heavy bull-hide chaps for our legs. Even with that help, at night each of us had to pick thorns and cactus from each others' legs. I felt sorry for our horses. They had the tough part, but we used liniment and salve on them too. Our job was better than the one Chaco and his crew had. We had the cattle in front of us to break the trail for us.

Just before dark that night, we could hear cattle bawling up ahead. We had covered about sixteen miles. If we were lucky, Chaco could hear the cattle also. The light breeze was blowing his direction, and I hoped he was not too far west. We heard a horse approaching, and it turned out to be one of the riders from Chaco. They heard the cattle and wanted us to come around and plan with Chaco. We were very happy to oblige.

About an hour later we were eating a fast meal of jerky, if you could call it a meal. Chaco opened the discussion by commenting on our good fortune to this point.

"Men, it may be that some of us will not live past tonight. I want all of you to know, if this ranch is to survive, it will be because of dedicated vaqueros. You and your families will be taken care of. Be careful, and make every shot count. Toady, I would like for you to take one man, and with bow and arrow, take out the first man or two you encounter. That way, we all can get closer to the herd."

He laid out a general plan for us to surround the herd and

each pick one man to attack. If they had no more than the few men they started with, we should have more men than they. We also had surprise on our side. They probably figured no one was following them. No doubt they would be liquored up by midnight, which was the agreed time for us to move in. Chaco would fire three shots rapidly as a signal.

I really did not like the idea of killing all the enemy, but I got to thinking of the two men who lost their lives a few nights ago at their camp. After all, the German brothers had declared war on Chaco's family and the Rattlesnake Ranch. We had no other choice if we were to survive. Later, the face of Rosita crossed my mind. I sure did want to get back and see her again. Maybe she would not be prejudiced against this *gringo*.

Shortly after midnight we heard the three shots and moved in rapidly, yellin' and shooting as we had planned. In about fifteen minutes, no more shootin' was heard, so we gradually circled around and all gathered at one spot.

"Looks like we got all eight of 'em," I said. Chaco backed me on that, and we had lost none, not even a wound.

He said, "That should convince them we mean business. Let's eat a good meal."

What he meant was, *Break out the jerky again*, since that is all we had. So we had a meal and turned in. Men were posted around the cattle, which had already bedded down in a grove of oak trees near a creek.

At daybreak we had the cattle on the move north to our ranch. It took two days to get to the property line on the south end. We crossed the Frio River and took them farther on the third day. José had already been sent to headquarters with the good news. Before the day was over, he came back on the run on a fresh horse. Me and Chaco met him.

"What is the matter, José?" Chaco asked. He rapidly spoke

in Spanish, and then Chaco told us the news. The German brothers had attacked two more camps on the west side and killed all five men at the two camps. Three rustlers also lost their lives. It was now open war.

After meeting for two hours and planning an attack, I decided it best to ride to Pearsall and wire the ranger's office. Chaco assured me the telegraph office was a safe place and it would take me all day to ride there and back, if I encountered no interference or bad weather. They saddled a fast, powerful sorrel mare for me, and the women gave me a cloth sack of food for two days.

The trip was tiring but otherwise- uneventful. The telegraph office was across the street from the sheriff's office. Billy Towson was the operator, and he had no real likes for the Germans in the area, but he did respect their needs, as he did ours.

"Be careful what you say in the bar if you go there. The sheriff has some good friends who hang around there, and he is close to the German families since he married a girl from one of them. I don't know as I would trust him very far."

"Thanks, Mr. Towson," I said.

"Just call me Billy. I prefer that. And be careful. And good luck in your quest. If you need me at any time of night, I live just one street back of here. The house with the two apple trees in the front."

I thanked him and said I would wait for an answer over in the bar, two stores down from the sheriff's office. I went over the street, leaving my horse where it was. In the bar I found only one cowboy seated at a back table, and I went to the bar for a visit with the bartender.

"Howdy do, sir. What can I get you?"

"I only need a mild drink like a sarsaparilla if you got one. Been kinda off my feed fer a day or two."

"Fresh out. Only got some water, if you can handle anything that strong."

"Guess I might."

He brought a coffee cup full, and since it had no wrigglers in it, I figured it might be safe enough. I thanked him and started for a seat.

"Don't know as I've seen you 'round here before, cowboy."

"I ain't from around here. That may be the reason." I headed on to a table to wait for a while.

A few minutes later, a young boy came in, and the bartender spoke to him and the boy walked out. In a few minutes, a tall, heavy-set man walked in wearing a star pinned to his vest. His pot belly stuck way out beyond his vest and hung over his belt. He walked over to my table, eyeing me all the way.

"Hear you smarted off to the bartender, cowboy."

"You must have good ears, Sheriff. Didn't know I was talkin' that loud."

"Don't smart off at me, boy. You could land in my jail."

"Didn't know I was smartin' off, Sheriff."

"Maybe I need to give you a lesson in talkin' while you're in my town."

"Oh!" I said. "Didn't know you were a Pearsall. I'll try to control my tongue."

"Not a Pearsall, but this is my town, and any more lip from you and you'll taste the food we serve, if you're able to taste by then."

"Whatever you say, Mr. Sheriff." I continued to drink the water and ignored him. After waiting for a full minute, he turned and walked to the bar and ordered a beer and brought it back to my table.

After he pulled out a chair and sat down, I said, "Why don't you have a seat, sir?"

"There you go again, cowboy. You're shorely tryin' my patience. One more word like that and I'll run you in."

I did not want to spend time in his jail, nor did I have time to fool with his power play, so I just nodded and went on drinking my water. After he took a couple more swigs of beer, he asked, "What brings you our way?"

"Up where I'm from, folks don't ask nosy questions, Sheriff."

"My business to be nosy. Been some trouble around here, and we don't like people comin' in here raisin' Cain. Mean to stay on top of it is all."

"Then I hope you are successful at it, Sheriff."

"You still owe me an answer. Where you from and why are you in my town?"

"I'm from Arkansas and jist passin' through here."

"How come you parked that sorrel across the street instead of here?"

"Didn't figure I needed to make a fast getaway, as I ain't robbin' a bank or nuthin'."

"Finish that drink and be on your way, cowboy."

"Cain't I even eat supper before I go?"

"Not today, you done wore out your welcome."

"Is this the way you welcome everyone who visits yore town, Mr. Sheriff?"

He did not like the tone of my voice—but chose to turn and walk out. I was glad. The bartender smiled at me and watched me leave.

When I went into the telegraph office, I was handed a printed message. I thanked Billy and put the paper in my shirt pocket, walked out the door, and mounted my horse. I went south and then angled back southwest toward the ranch. It would be late when I got there, so I stopped and looked in the sack for something to eat. I got home after midnight and was greeted by two of our guards. One of them recognized me and welcomed me back. He introduced me to another Chaco, who was a distant cousin to the ranch owner.

The next morning, I arose early and met Chaco, Tab, and the others for breakfast. I shared the news from the ranger captain. He had told me to go ahead as planned and attack the German ranch. He planned to join us just before we got there and would have about ten rangers with him. We were greatly encouraged.

We each loaded our saddlebags with shells, both pistol and rifle. Most of us had a rifle that fired forty-fours like our pistols, so that caused less confusion and allowed each to carry more shells.

The trail north to the ranch border was rather brushy, along with some boulders that afforded cover for us as well as ideal places for an ambush, so we had to be alert at all times. The distance was over twenty-five miles, which took us several hours. Each of us had two horses, which we would need if we were to be successful. We planned it that way and would not settle for anything less. Enough was enough, or as Tab expressed it, "Nuff sed!"

Before leaving the ranch headquarters, Chaco had men from neighboring ranches gathered to guard the houses and barns in case the ruthless brothers used this time to try to burn us out. Fortunately, he was a man of good report in the whole area, and several white ranchers joined in his effort to protect his property. Chaco would see that they were well-rewarded.

Chaco and I rode ahead after a short noon break to scout the area. The small town of Frio, called Frio Town, was about four or five miles north of our ranch border and was on the Frio River. We decided to wait for the other men to catch up, and then we sent Toady and one of Chaco's men to the river to approach the town from that side. Another of his men took Tab to the west side of the town to enter from there. Chaco and I rode toward the ranch of one of the largest spreads in the whole area. It would make two of the size Chaco owned.

The rancher had seven daughters, and all of them were home when we got there. His name was Slaughter, and he did not appreciate the attitude of the German brothers. He had known them and their families for a number of years. He would not allow his daughters to dance with any of the German boys at the functions they attended.

We were invited in and were given cool drinks of a special tea the girls had brewed. It was made from cactus and had a good taste. He told us to come across his land anytime we needed to and to always send for help if need be.

"Señor Slaughter, you have known my father for many years and know that he always respected you. I have the same feelings," Chaco said.

"Yes, Chaco. We visited many times over the years and helped one another during hard work times together. I want us to continue this relationship, if you so desire."

"I certainly do and will help you if you will allow us when needed."

"Do you need some more men? I can spare fifteen or twenty for a few days."

"Gracias, Señor Slaughter. We have some help coming up the road before we get to D'Hanis. A group of Texas Rangers will be coming from Austin."

"You could not have a better bunch of men on your side. A cousin of mine is a ranger in northwest Texas. I wish he could be with you. He is a fightin' dude."

I was impressed by the sincerity of Mr. Slaughter. I was

more than slightly impressed by the beauty of one of his daughters. I think her name was Dottie, which was a shortened version of Dorothy. I made a vow to return to the ranch and call on her when times got better.

The girls were on the porch when we rode away. One of the girls waved to us as we looked back. I think it was Dottie, and Chaco teased me about her. I didn't mind a bit.

We made good time going north from the Slaughter ranch. We rode west of the community of Yancey, not wanting to alert anyone who might be a friend of the German brothers. About five miles southeast of D'Hanis we met the rangers. They had a camp set up in a very secluded area on a creek about three miles west of Hondo.

That night, Chaco asked the sergeant of the rangers to map out a plan to use and an alternate one. After a good meal of chili and beans, we bedded down for the night. The next morning at dawn, Chaco and I headed northeast toward Boerne, and the others went due north toward Fredricksburg. At the widest point we would be no farther apart than six miles, which would allow either to send word of any confrontation. We were to meet about three miles east of Comfort on the Guadalupe River. It should take no longer than three days.

Before we had ridden two miles, a rider came at a gallop from our west. It was Tab. Chaco and I rode out to meet him.

"We had to stop and hide west of here about three miles," he said. "There was a large number of riders, perhaps as many as twelve headin' south. They are heavily armed with rifles and pistols."

"What word come with you about what we should do?" the Sergeant asked.

"Your ranger lieutenant wanted us to ride southwest

and intercept them about where the west boundary of the Slaughter Ranch West Camp is. He suggested we also get Mr. Slaughter to send some of his men, since it would be on or near his ranch."

"Good idea," Chaco said. "Do you need a fresh horse?"

"Not yet. Mine hasn't been pushed too hard."

Later that day we met up with the others and made our plans. I agreed to ride to the Slaughter Ranch headquarters to alert them. I wondered if I would be able to see the prettiest daughter. Sure hoped so, but told no one.

The Slaughter hands were ready to go in thirty minutes, and we were to find the path the invaders were taking so we could come in behind them. That was not hard because the riders were familiar with all the trails used on the ranch. We had ridden two miles north before turning west to the Leona River. It might soon be over, and Chaco could get on with his ranch life as usual. We all hoped for his sake this was the case. He had been through too much from the German brothers and their men.

Before we got to the river, one of the Slaughter hands cautioned us to ride wide-awake. Their line camp was just over the next rise and would likely be the place where we met the others and the German crooks. In case I hadn't told you, the German brothers were Karl and Hermann Zimmer. Karl was the older, and according to stories about them, he was the most vile and dangerous. We checked our pistols and rifles for about the hundred time each. It helped to soothe our nerves.

Gunfire erupted before we got over the rise, so we stepped up the pace. When we got near the top, Bob Taft of the Slaughter Ranch went first and quickly turned and said, "It's our men, and they are trapped in the small line shack. They're getting ready to set it on fire!"

We hurried and started shooting into the bunch closest to us. They were only about five hundred yards away. When we opened fire, one of the men setting the fire mounted and rode north in a hurry. I followed and took the rifle, aimed at his horse, and fired. The horse dove headfirst into a heavy brushy area. His rider fell under it.

One ranger and I quickly went to the spot and saw that he was knocked out or dead. We hoped for the first. We wanted a live prisoner. That's what we got. As we pulled him from the briar patch, we saw that he had severe scratches all over his face and hands. He also had some thorns sticking into his face. I started to pull them out, but Ranger Joe Cantrell said, leave them in for now. I wondered why but said nothing.

Later, I realized why. When he began to recover, he was cursing us in German. Ranger Joe told him, "Sir, if you value your life, you will speak American and not that gibberish you been slingin' at us." He looked at us as though he didn't understand, but then he said in a broken English, "Vy do you not pull these oudt? They hurting me are."

"You'll have to speak better'n that. I don't understand you," Ranger Joe said.

"Me neither," I put in.

"What is the meaning of this? Why did you kill my horse?" he said very clearly.

"We'll tell you the answer to that when you explain why you were running away from the fight back yonder and why you and your men were trying to kill the Mexican families at Rattlesnake Ranch."

"I don't know anything about a fight and anybody killing anybody," he said.

It was obvious that he was lying. "What are you going to do to me?" he asked.

"I haven't made my mind up yet. Suppose you start walking back the way you were running from while we decide. Now, move out."

Chapter 14

It was only about three miles to the camp, but it took almost three hours to get there. The land was rough and had a lot of scrub brush, oak, and rocks to get over and around. Our German friend grumbled all the way back.

We heard no gunshots, so we assumed it was over. It was. Tab and Luis came to meet us. They were happy to report complete success but would not explain. They wanted to let the ranger captain give the details. We helped the German pull the thorns from his face. He took his shirt and pants off and had about fifty or more under those. No wonder he grumbled all the way back.

"I'd sure enough grumble if I had to walk three miles with my skin punctured like his," I said.

We had a good meal prepared by Tab and his two Mexican assistants. Even the captive ate a lot. However, he refused to say anything when asked his name or what he was doing in the area. Ranger Cantrell continued to threaten him with torture unless he cooperated. He still refused to respond.

Cantrell said, "I'll take him to Austin and he'll talk. Prepare a horse for him early tomorrow and we'll head out. I believe this problem is over anyway."

The next morning, as we were getting ready to mount up, a voice came from the brush, "Hello, the camp. This is Ranger Captain Burl Maxey. I'd like to come in."

Ranger Cantrell answered for him to ride on in. He was welcomed by his men along with the riders from the Rattlesnake Ranch. Me and Tab and Toady waited until all the others had greeted him before we spoke up.

"Sir," I said, "this is Tab, Toady, and me you met in Austin over two or three months ago."

"How are you, Mr. Buckskin Bradley? Good to see all you boys again. What are you doing with the baby Zimmer brother?"

"We are fine now, but it hasn't always been that way. Had a lot of problems with some people attacking us. Ranger Cantrell can explain what he knows, and we'll fill in the rest. Have you met Chaco Cardenas?"

"Not yet. Is this him?"

"It sure is, Captain Maxey. We are glad to have you on our humble rancho."

"Where were you taking this rat who thinks he owns Texas? Is he the one causing all the problems?"

"I'll fill you in, Captain," Ranger Cantrell said. "Have you had anything to eat?"

"Not since last night. I stopped at Slaughter Ranch for supper, and he told me of some of the events."

We dismounted and began to prepare a bite for him. That is, Tab did. The most unusual thing happened then. Captain Maxey asked the Zimmer brother where his brother was, and he denied having a brother. Then Captain Maxey said, "Chaco, where is the biggest oak tree around this area?"

"Just a mile from here, near the Rio Leona is a large grove of tall oaks."

"Good, as soon as I eat, we'll take him there and stretch his neck. Somebody put a lariat around his neck now so he'll get used to the feel of it. I've been wanting to catch him and his brother for a long time. I'm tired of their lying and stealing."

I moved closer and put one around his neck. It was a "hangman's knot," with thirteen wraps around the rope below the loop that goes over the head. One of the rangers had prepared it while we were talking.

Young Zimmer said, "You can't do this to me. It is not right. I have done nothing."

Ranger Cantrell brought a young German boy about fifteen years old to face him.

"Karl, do you know the man with the rope around his neck?"

"If I tell you, will you let me go? My father will be worried about me."

"You have the same first name as Karl Zimmer. Are you related to him?" Captain Maxey asked.

"No, sir, I ain't no kin, but he is the younger brother to Karl."

"This boy can go home. Somebody find him a horse and saddle."

The young boy thanked him along with a promise to stay away from the older Karl Zimmer.

"Now," Captain Maxey said, "back to the current problem. Do you still claim to be innocent?"

Zimmer continued to stare at the ground or glare into the face of the ranger captain.

"Okay, men, let's find those oak trees."

It took us about thirty minutes to cover the mile, and all the while, Zimmer rode quietly. When we got there, Ranger Cantrell rode over to a tall oak with a strong, straight branch about ten or twelve feet off the ground. He yelled and motioned us over. I wondered if the hanging was really going to take place. We were about to find out.

Ranger Cantrell took the loose end of the hangman's rope and threw it over the limb. He then loosed the loop from around Hermann Zimmer's neck, put the rope through the small loop of the loose end, and pulled it tight around the limb. He placed the loop around Zimmer's neck and snugged it again.

Ranger Captain Maxey said to him, "Any last requests before you stretch this thing?"

"You got no cause to do this to me. I haven't hurt anyone."

"I guess you claim no responsibility in the slaughter of about twenty to thirty vaqueros from this one ranch, burning their buildings, or killing other ranchers and taking over their ranches?"

"You are crazy to think I had anything to do with that."

With a slight nod of his head toward one of the rangers, the corporal rode up behind Zimmer's horse and slapped it on the rump. Zimmer yelled and began kicking his legs as we watched his life leave his body. In a few minutes one of the men lifted him as another removed the hangman's knot. It had really happened. I witnessed my first hanging and had that same funny feeling in my gut that I had when my ma died a few years earlier.

Captain Maxey said, "Men, you who are new to this country have just got a taste of 'Frontier Justice,' and even though it seems cruel, it is effective. Hermann Zimmer will never cause anymore problems."

There were no replies, as each of us had to wrastle with our own feelings. I fully intended to ask Captain Maxey if I was to deal with crooks the same way. I really didn't know if I could. I'm sure some of the others felt the same. I sure hoped I'd never have to make that choice.

Captain Maxey wanted the body taken to the Zimmer Ranch, so Toady and me said we would ride to the Slaughter Ranch and borrow a wagon. Tab agreed, reluctantly, to wait with two rangers to guard the body. Chaco and his hands went back to their places. The hands from the Slaughter Ranch rode with me and Toady.

Toady knew why I wanted to go to the Slaughter place. It had to do with Dottie Slaughter. I wanted to ask one of the cowboys about her but was afraid she might belong to one of them. I'd find out in a day or two if she was at home.

When we got to the Slaughter line the next day, we were met by four riders. I sure hoped it was not the Zimmer gang. It wasn't. It was Mr. Slaughter, two cowboys, and one cowgirl. Sure enough, the big smile I got was from Dottie. I was elated. We were welcomed along with the riders from the ranch and could not wait to share the good news. I let the rangers with us tell the whole story as soon we got to the main headquarters.

The daughters served us some cold tea they had brewed. I listened to make sure the rangers told the whole story and all agreed not to tell anyone about the hanging. Captain Maxey wanted the older Karl Zimmer to sweat for a few days when his younger brother did not come back.

Mr. Slaughter said, "I sure thank all of you for what you did." Then he promised to ride with us if we decided to attack the Zimmer Ranch. He had lost some close friends who were small ranchers and had their places stolen by the Zimmers. His attitude was that "right would always win out," even though it sometimes took a long time.

"Hermann Zimmer was like a snake in tall grass. He needed to be defanged, and you men did the job for all of us. The young boy named Karl Zimmer came by here. His horse had a bad leg, and I let him have one that he promised to return as soon as he could. He told us about the hanging and seemed glad of it."

We thanked them for the loan of the wagon and team, and I had noticed that every time I looked up at Dottie, she was smiling at me. I sure took that as a good sign and promised myself I would come back and see her soon. She even walked up to the wagon and told me good-bye and asked me if I would call on her sometime.

I told her, "Yes, ma'am, I surely will. As soon as I can git loose."

Chapter 15

Me and Toady rode the rough wagon back to the camp where the hangin' took place. We had a lot to talk about on the way but were glad to git back. It was almost dark of the second day, so we got ready to bed down. The men were happy to see us and reported no problems while we were gone.

Tab asked, "Was the pretty daughter there, Toady?"

He replied, "You shore asked the wrong one. Tell 'im, Buck."

"She shore was and asked me to come see her soon," I said. They hoorahed me fer the rest of the evening. It made me proud too.

The next morning, Tab had a good breakfast of eggs, bacon, and black coffee fer us that would last all day. We loaded the body of Hermann Zimmer in the wagon. It had been wrapped in heavy canvas tarp that the Slaughters' foreman thought about letting us use. Hermann's body was gettin' ripe by this time and would smell before dark tonight. We wasted no time on the trip north. On the way, Tab drove the wagon while Toady and me rode up front a ways, and the two rangers rode about half a mile on both sides of us. We had no trouble, but the next day would likely be different, especially when we got near Zimmer Ranch.

It was different, and we did have some trouble. About five miles from our destination, a group of eight riders approached from the northwest. We pulled up and got our rifles and pistols out so they'd be handy. As the riders approached, they began to separate, so we could not cover all of them at once. We were aware that might happen, so we already had a plan if shooting started.

Two of the riders came closer, and one asked, "Who are you and what you want here?"

Ranger Sergeant Meadows said, "We'll answer that when you tell us who you are and why you are so impolite."

"I'll impolite you, so tell me who you are."

"Texas Rangers. Now who're you?"

"What you rangers want here?"

Sergeant Meadows said, "You haven't said who you are."

"None of yer business. 'Sides, yer on our property. Now git back where ye come from or tell us what ye want."

"Whose property?"

"Zimmer Brothers, smarty, now what ye want?"

"Thought we might let you know this is no longer Zimmer Brothers' property."

"What do ye mean by that? Answer me quick."

Sergeant Meadows said, "For your information, there is only one Zimmer now, not two. We have the dead one here in this wagon, which we wanted to deliver home, but will dump him here. You take him home."

"What do ye mean 'dead one'? What happened to 'im?"

"We found him two days ago hanging from a tall oak tree on the banks of the Leona River, and a young boy knew him so we decided to bring him here. Buck, you and Toady dump him out so we can go."

"Wait a minute! You'll not be dumpin' him 'til ye git 'im on to the main house. It's about four miles due north of here. We'll foller. How do we know it's him?"

"Glad for you to look see, only one at a time to identify him. You first," Sergeant Meadows said, pointing to the one who had been talking. He dismounted, walked over, and pulled the tarp back on one end. Only his boots were showing, so he went to the other side and removed some cover. He grabbed his nose and backed away quickly.

"It's Hermann!"

"Now cover him back like you found him," the sergeant said.

The cowboy obeyed but still frowned. The other cowboys had slowly come in closer for a look. The other ranger nodded to Buck and the others and then gave an order for the German ranch hands to drop their weapons. They all looked up quickly and saw pistols pointing at them. Each one took a weapon and dropped it to the ground.

"Now," Sergeant Meadows ordered, "dismount one at a time and move away on foot. Slowly, starting with you," he said, pointing at a big-bellied man on the left. He did, and another followed until all were on the ground.

Buck got the leather thong from the wrapped body of Hermann Zimmer and told the men to turn around and cross their hands behind their backs. They did, and Toady, along with Tab, began a thorough job of tying each securely. Their horses were left to find the way back to ranch headquarters. The men were ordered to line up single file from the shortest to the tallest while a loop of lariat was placed on each neck, secured by a thong of leather.

"Okay, you jerks, slowly walk toward the ranch headquarters. The first man to yell a warning gets a bullet through his gut. Got that?" Sergeant Meadows said. We lined up on both sides from front to rear and walked by them all the four miles. The men wanted to stop for various reasons, but we did not allow it. One of them even wet his pants, but Ranger Maxey made the motion to keep moving. I'll tell a man, they were mighty upset.

As we approached the buildings of the main ranch, two cowboys came out of the bunk house and got on their horses and slowly walked toward us. They were not wearing pistols. As they got closer, one of them asked, "What's the meaning of this? Who are you?"

Sergeant Meadow answered, "Do you know these men?" A quick reply came in the form of a German slang word. Meadow told him to answer in English.

"They work here. What do you mean tying them like this?"

Sergeant Meadow thought for a little and said, "I want to see Karl Zimmer now!"

They said he was not on the ranch and would not be back for two days. Sergeant Meadow told the one who had been talking that he and his other man could unload the body from the wagon. They walked over to it and looked startled.

"That's Hermann. What did you do to him? Why are these men tied up?"

Sergeant Meadow told them that Hermann had been hung for murder and resisted arrest after running away from a sneak attack on the Rattlesnake Ranch.

"We are taking these men on to Austin since they were arrested after being captured at the same battle that Hermann ran away from. You can tell Karl Zimmer the Texas Rangers have them now and will hold them for trial. If he wants them, he will need to come unarmed to see Captain Burl Maxey in Austin. Now, get that body from the wagon so we can load these men and go."

"You can't treat these men like this all the way to Austin. That's over sixty miles."

"We can, and we will. One of you go get enough jerky to last them all the way. Now get moving," Sergeant Meadows said. One of the men went at a fast pace to the bunk house and came back with a sack of jerky and handed it to Tab. The look he gave Tab would have stopped a big clock. Tab just smiled.

They unloaded the body onto the ground and backed away from the odor.

"Is that all?" he asked in a sarcastic tone.

"No, one of you mount that horse tied to the rail of the bunk house and lead us to the best trail to Austin."

He did, and we loaded the men into the wagon and followed him almost due east off their ranch.

We followed the trail for about two miles and stopped for a short breather for the horses.

"Sergeant, aren't we playing a dangerous game by letting him tell us the best trail to follow?" I asked.

He replied, "That is what I want him to think. I know this country as well or better than he does. I was reared just a few miles from this very spot and have been over just about every trail there is from here to Austin. As soon as it gets dark, we'll move north about two miles and spend the night and then take off in a northeasterly direction. That'll take us a little north of Austin, but a safe way to go. The trail I want is much better and safer, even though it is longer."

"Do you expect Karl to attack us on the way?" I asked.

"Not likely, but we'll watch out for him. He'll probably bury his brother and then try to decide what to do. After all, he's lost a lot of his toughest men. It may not be easy to hire many more around here. It's time to mount up and move north. There is a small creek near here that we can follow north."

We did and found the creek and went to bed, if you could call it that. One at a time we unloaded the men and let them relieve themselves. When one got through, another one got out of the wagon. They were allowed to bed down next to each other but still had their hands tied behind their backs.

It started raining before morning, and the prisoners complained all the way to Austin. We had nothing available to warm them or keep them dry. At least the tracks we left were rained out, so the danger of being found lessened considerably. I was sure glad of that and the others were too. We made it to Austin the next day about noon and deposited the prisoners in the jail. Captain Maxey greeted us warmly.

Chapter 16

I had several good visits with Captain Maxey over the next few days. He had a lot of plans ready for me, along with a new appointment for Tab, which wasn't easy since not many Negroes were in law enforcement in the south. He also had a special appointment for Toady, which came from the governor's office. We were really excited, especially when we all learned that money for the three of us had been approved for the next year.

"Here's the way I have it, men. Tab, you and Toady will be assigned to work under Corporal Buck Bradley. Each of you will be provided with two horses, a rifle, pistol, holster, and shells for each gun. Wear the badges with honor and make Texas proud."

I could hardly believe the promotion to corporal, but Ranger Meadows had given us a glowing report to Captain Maxey about the events at Chaco's ranch. I could hardly wait to get to Slaughter Ranch and tell Dottie, but that would have to wait. The Zimmer hands' trial was coming up, and all three of us would have to be available to testify. We were scared out of our wits, but all the rangers told us not to worry. We were not the ones on trial. For that we were glad.

We went out for target practice about a week later. Toady took to the rifle like a duck on a June bug. He beat Tab by several points but still did not come close to my score. The pistol practice was about even between them and not far behind me. Captain Maxey told us how pleased he was with our progress.

"Monday I want all three of you to stay around close in town. Word on the street is that Karl Zimmer is coming in next Monday. He is very mad because his innocent little brother was hanged. I don't want any of you to confront him without other rangers with you."

"Why us, sir? Does he know about me being a ranger?" I asked.

"It appears someone let it out that you are a ranger, and he knows about you three being on the ranch together. Looks as if we have somebody around here looking to be fired. I sure hope that's not the case, but don't be caught alone," he said.

"What do you suggest we do then?" I wanted to know.

"I'll assign each of you to another ranger until this thing is over. Don't go on the street without your partner, is that clear?"

We all agreed it was. Monday came and went without incident, and each of us was listening for any clue as to who it was that spoke out of turn and let Karl know.

Maybe it was just rumor. Anyway, we were ready. On Thursday Captain Maxey called me into his office. He handed me a letter that had followed me for several weeks. I was surprised, as I had never gotten one before. Turned out to be from Toby.

I tore it open as soon as I got out of his office. It was bad news. Big tears came into my eyes as I read it:

> We got here and started a gold-mining job. We found a good place up in this mountain where gold had been found. After about two weeks, Pa had a bag full of nuggets and dust, and one night he was attacked by robbers who stole it and killed him. Nobody saw it, and I did not know where to turn. Mr. Story had gone on to his rondevoo, so he doesn't know about it. I buried Pa on this mountain. I didn't know what to do except to cash in my gold and head back home. By the time you git this letter, I should be back there. Write me ...
>
> Toby

Tab came in and seen I'd been cryin' and wanted to know what was wrong. I told him and tears watered his eyes too. That made it worse for me. He wanted to head fer Colorado and find the killers fer me and Toby.

"Tab, that'll have to wait. Toby won't even be there, and we wouldn't know where to go or who to see," I said.

It was a miserable feelin' I had in my gut. Jist like the ones I had when Mom died or when me and Julie was together. Julie? I hadn't thought about her in a long time. I hoped she never found out. Boy, was I gittin' in over my head. First, there was Julie Benton at home, then a pretty girl over at Jefferson. What was her name? Milly Morgan? Then Chaco's beautiful sister at the ranch, and now Dottie Slaughter. How many more would there be? A guy can dream, I guess. I reminded myself to write to Toby when I could find the right time. I read his letter again before going to bed.

Ranger Meadows offered to buy us a beer in a bar down the street. I had never had a beer and asked Tab and Toady if they had. Neither had, but we went to give it a try. The beer was cold and had a bitter taste that I did not like and could not understand why anyone else would. I could understand how one cowboy had said, "If you don't like it, you can always pour it back in the horse." Now I know what he meant. I asked for a milder drink and got a sarsaparilla, which was sweet and tasted better.

While we were in the bar, a group of loud cowboys came in and demanded service. Sergeant Meadows put a finger to his lips and whispered to us, "The big man in the black cowboy hat is Karl Zimmer. Let's go out quietly and report to Captain Maxey."

As we were almost out the door, a loud shout called us back.

"Where y'all goin'? We need some information. I heard they wuz a ranger nest in this here town, and I'm here to destroy their play purty."

Sergeant Meadows told him to go north about one block and the office was on the same side of the street. The black-hatted cowboy replied, "How 'bout you walkin' up there with me? I'm afraid in this here town by myself." All his men gave out a big guffaw. We noted the two guns on his hips. Captain Maxey had told Zimmer's man to have him come in unarmed.

"I'll be glad to escort you up there. Come on." He proceeded toward the door. I had already beat him out and Tab also. I told Tab to run ahead and alert the others. He did.

Karl Zimmer said, "Come on, boys. Let's see what a ranger nest looks like."

They got up to leave, with Ranger Meadows in the lead, followed by Karl Zimmer. Two of his men were next, but

Toady and I moved in front of them so we could follow Karl Zimmer. We got some dirty looks, but no one said anything. The others followed.

As we entered the large reception room, only one ranger was at a desk. He asked if he could be of service, and Ranger Meadows moved to one side of Karl Zimmer and spoke.

"Corporal, these men would like to see Captain Maxey."

"Yes, sir. I'll go get him for you." He left the room. I noticed a side door open, and Tab, along with three other rangers, came in and walked to the back wall and down the side a ways. I felt some relief. That evened up the odds considerably. About that time the door opened and Captain Maxey walked in. When all the men looked at him, Toady and I moved closer to Karl, and each of us took a pistol from his holsters. He looked around to say something and looked into the barrel of my pistol.

"Karl Zimmer, you are under arrest for murder. Raise your hands and tell your men to do the same. Now!" I said.

Each of the rangers had pistols pointing at the men. They were all somewhat flabbergasted at how easily we had tricked them. By this time six more rangers had come in. Five more were at the front door and four were in the back. We had them corralled. They gave up without a fight.

"What's the meaning of this? We came here in peace to see why my brother was hung without a trial and you locked up all my men." He acted very distraught, and I supposed he was.

Captain Maxey told one of the rangers near him to get two men to help gather up the firearms and two others to handcuff the prisoners. Behind their backs, too.

Then he answered Karl Zimmer. "You have been a menace in this area and all the way to the Rio Grande. We have grown tired of your killing and stealing ranches all around. It will not be tolerated by the people of this state."

"You ain't got no proof of what you say."

"We have written statements from seven of your men who were in on the latest attempt to grab the Rattlesnake Rancho from Chaco Cardenas. Also, we have statements from four ranchers you tried to kill but survived even though you took their places. That is plenty of evidence. See you in hell, Karl Zimmer. Sergeant Meadows, escort these gentlemen down Main Street to the jail and lock them up. Give Karl Zimmer a separate cell away from the others and put them all in one cell if they'll fit. If not, use two."

"Yes, sir, Captain. Okay, men, walk out the front door and turn left."

They did, and we escorted a bunch of angry men to jail.

Chapter 17

We took three days on the trip back to the ranch. I wanted to look for a present for Rosita and one for Dottie Slaughter. I hoped one of them would be glad to see me. I also took a lot of kiddin' from my friends. When we finally got home, we were a tired but happy bunch. A good hot bath and a soft bunk would be mighty welcomed by all of us. We did not even eat supper but went to work heating water for the bath. That galvanized tub got a real workout that night.

The next morning Chaco told us to mount up. He had a chore for us at one of the line camps. He refused to tell us what it was, so we saddled up and rode out as soon as breakfast was over. The line camp was ten miles south, and when we got there, a tall cowboy met us. It turned out to be the John Blocker we had met at the west line camp where the battle was several days ago.

Chaco said, "Señor Blocker, these three rowdy cowboys think they are good cowhands. How about you show them how to make a loop for these Longhorn cattle?"

"Hi, men," he said. "I'll be glad to. Tell me again who each one is so I can remember."

We each told him our name. He began by mounting his horse and untying his lariat. It appeared to be the longest rope I had ever seen, even though I hadn't seen many. He slung the small loop slowly on his right side, and we watched as the loop got bigger and bigger. He was talking all the time the loop was moving.

"As you kin see, we need a big loop fer the wide horns. This reata is only sixty-five feet long, but I have one about ninety feet at home. I want you to see how to do this little one first. The trick is to get the loop goin' as you ride, and as you pick up speed nearin' the steer or cow, you gradually lift the reata up and over yore head so you kin throw it over the horns of the steer."

Chaco told two of his hands from the line camp to bring a steer from the pen. In a couple of minutes they had one down and ready to go.

Chaco said, "You men are about to witness what is known in South Texas as the 'John Blocker Loop.'"

The men were all lined around, so Luis told us to open up and try to run the steer west. We moved so that was possible, and John Blocker now had a small loop in his reata. The steer was turned loose with a slap on his rump as he got up. He lit out of there at a fast pace with John Blocker right behind. The steer tried to veer off to the left, so Mr. Blocker moved over a little to the left, and the steer ran faster. So did the Blocker gelding. The reata was now big enough, it looked like to us, and sure enough, it started up and over his head. Now, John Blocker was right on top of the steer and about twenty feet behind it. The loop went out and settled gently over the front of the steer, around both horns, and John Blocker signaled his horse to stop. It did, and the reata drew snug around the neck and the steer flipped back and over. Before it could recover, two vaqueros who had been trailing on horses jumped off and ran to the head and rear of the steer. One put his knee on the neck right behind the head and the other grabbed the top right leg and pulled it back toward the rear while the vaquero's right boot jammed above the knee of the left leg on the ground.

Chaco said, "That is the same position we use to brand the calves. It is easy when you learn how."

"That looks easy enough. When do we get to try it?" I asked.

We had all given a big hand clap for the roping demonstration, and he smiled and said, "Tomorrow I will come to the headquarter ranch and start the lessons. It'll take a while before you'll try it like I did with a long reata. After you learn how, you'll appreciate this loop like I do. It saves a lot of work in this scrub oak country."

We thanked him, and with that he rode west to his ranch. We rode on south to another line camp to check on things there. It was near dark when we got back home, tired but happy about our prospects. I could hardly wait 'til morning.

The next two nights we sat around a fire outside while some of the vaqueros sang and played an instrument that must have been a forerunner of our guitars. They really could sing, but it was in Spanish, which few of us understood. It was still pretty music. Then Rosita and two of her girlfriends sang and danced to the tune of *La Cucaracha*. They also sang it in American, which was *The Cockroach*. It was really cute, and I told Rosita I sure did like it. I noticed that both nights every time I glanced at her she would blush and look away.

I had to find some way to get her alone, but that is hard to do considering the Spanish way of an older woman always escorting or chaperoning a younger girl in the presence of a male suitor.

Later on one day, I saw her alone when I rode up to the corral and started to pen my horse. She motioned for me to go into the barn. I did, and she met me just inside the barn. Boy, it was my lucky day. She put her arms around my neck, pulled my head down, and planted a really juicy kiss. It must've been a full ten minutes long, but it was probably only a few seconds. She told me there were plenty more where that one came from, and she would plan a way for me to escort her on a trail ride around part of the ranch. I got really excited and told her I'd be happy to take her anywhere.

Just then, the barn door opened and two vaqueros and Chaco walked in. They were surprised to see us, but by the time their eyes adjusted to the indoor lighting, I was nearly to the stall with my horse and Rosita was still near the door. She carried the conversation with Chaco, and I only listened as well as I could from forty or more feet away.

Chaco said, "My little sister, what are you doing in the barn with this gringo?"

"He is no gringo. He is the one who saved you from the bad man on your trip to Washington. And here you refer to him as a common gringo. You should be ashamed of yourself, mi hermano."

"Right you are, mi hermana, but you did not answer my question."

"I was only showing him a clean stall for his caballo. Is that not permissible?"

"Okay for this time. Next time get a chaperone to help."

"Buck, I need to talk to you. Come on to the house as soon and you finish with your horse."

I did and went to the house. Chaco greeted me with a big smile, which told me that he was not mad at me for being alone with Rosita. I took that as a good sign. We sat at a table, and he told me some startling news. Karl Zimmer had escaped jail. He handed me a letter from Captain Maxey. I opened it.

> This letter will explain what we know about the escape of Karl Zimmer. Remember the day when I told you he knew you were a ranger? The man I suspected was the guilty one was the one who got him out. Apparently, he bribed the jailor and they let him out. None of his men got out. We think he may have headed for the Nueces Strip but will not know for sure for two or three weeks. I want you and Toady and Tab to stay on where you are until we confirm this. Just be ready to ride when you hear from us.

It was signed by Captain Maxey. I let Chaco read it since he already knew about the three of us being rangers.

"Also, John Blocker could not come for a few days due to some problems on his ranch. He should be here tomorrow or the next day. In the meantime, I want all of you to come to the barn where the tack room is. We will need to be there in about an hour."

I told him we'd be there and went to the stable. I had no idea what he wanted but figured it was important.

When we entered the stable area, a table had been moved out in the center. On the table were three cowhides and about four knives. One of the vaqueros, I think he was Luis or his brother, began talking and picked up a knife.

"I want each of you to get a knife and one of the hides. If you'll look at what I'm doing, that is what I want each of you to do. You will make some bad cuts, but if you are careful and take your time, I want you to cut three strands of leather about fifty feet long. After you get them cut, let me know and I'll show you the next step."

By this time I had guessed what we were doing. He was showing us how to weave one of the reatas we were to practice roping with. These men were very intelligent, even though most had never gone to school. We were impressed.

It took me almost two hours to get one strand that was long enough. My hand was already cramping from holding the knife so tight. I guessed the others were also having the same problem. We took a short break to feed and water our horses and then went back to the hides. I spent the rest of the day on the other two strands. Toady had his finished long before I did, and Tab was only a short time behind me.

Luis then showed us how to attach the three strands to a post about waist high. Then he took the strands and separated them between his fingers of one hand, and with the other hand he began lacing them, one over the other, being careful to place the correct one over the other. Every few twists he would pull them tight and make them look kind of rounded, like a finished rope. After he got the reata to about five feet, he dipped his hand into a bucket of lard and rubbed it on the reata so none was dripping off. He would pull the reata tight as he rubbed it. Even though he made it look easy, it was hard work. We went to bed tired that night and did not hang around for the singing after we ate.

"I got you beat, Buck," Toady said. "My reata is already two feet long. I'll finish it long before you will."

"That's because you are better with that knife, but I'll make up fer it when we throw the thangs, you wait and see."

Tab also complimented him on his fast work at cutting the strands. Toady had not messed up even once. Me and Tab ruined about three each. One of mine was almost twenty-seven feet long when I made a bad cut and had to start over.

I had to give both of them credit for beating me so bad on the cutting part, but I vowed to get even. Later that night, I told them about the letter from Captain Maxey and what he wanted us to do. Both were as upset as I was that a ranger had betrayed us to Karl Zimmer and helped him escape.

The next day we finished making the reatas and stretched them with as much force as we could. Luis was very pleased that we caught on as quickly as we did. I could hardly wait to show off my roping skills to Rosita.

John Blocker came in the morning of the next day, and we had a super good time all day as he instructed us on the proper way to use "the big loop," as he called it. There were plenty of mess-ups among the new ropers too. I was one of them. Toady actually outperformed all of us, including some of Chaco's vaqueros, who were good at throwing a reata.

"Just don't expect to become proficient at this for a while. It took me near a year to throw a seventy-foot one with any degree of success," John Blocker said.

Tab asked me what "proficient" meant, and I told him it was good or accurate. He nodded and smiled. We practiced for about an hour each day, usually after we finished work late in the day. Rosita came out to watch us every day that we threw the loops. She got a chance to laugh along with the rest of us every time we missed a calf. It's a good thing Chaco had a large number of calves and we each had four or five horses to rope from. I favored a big *grulla,* which, I was told, was a mouse-colored gelding. It was the best one of my horses.

Rosita would always leave just before we finished each time. I guess it was part of her culture, even though I preferred she stick around longer. We had been practicing for near a month, and Chaco told us to rest up for a big time this coming Saturday. He had set up a "challenge roping" for that day. Each one was given the opportunity to rope five calves, and we all drew for our times to rope. I had the third run on the first round. There were eight of us in the contest, and each round called for a different order to rope. That way, no one was given the best or worst place in the order. We anxiously awaited Saturday.

Saturday morning after breakfast we all assembled at the arena area with our first horse saddled and ready to run. The other four were tied to a long tie rail near the arena. That way, we didn't have to ride clear back to the stable for another horse. I was about to get used to the term *caballo,* which meant "horse" in Spanish. I was beginning to learn a little of the language each day.

By the time the first calf was run into the arena, there was a big crowd assembled. Chaco had invited as many hands as possible to be there from all the camps on the ranch. Many had their wives or girlfriends. It made for a great day. Luis was the first to ride, and he missed his calf. He was not the only one; in fact, only one calf in the first go was caught and that was by the hind legs. Renaldo's loop was big, and he failed to pull back until the calf was halfway through the loop. We gave him a big pat on the back for his throw.

The second round went about like the first. My reata went over one horn, and the steer veered away and the reata fell to the ground. Toady and Tab did no better. One of the vaqueros had better luck with a good throw, and his steer was caught just right. When he set the horse, the steer went over backward, and we ran to grab his legs and head before he could get up. The vaquero was from one of the camps south of us. His name was Rio.

The next two rounds were no different, but the last one was the one I liked. I finally had a good throw, and the reata sailed perfect and the steer was thrown. The rest of the boys almost caught theirs, but Tab came closest. On the last round, Toady came closer than the vaqueros. Chaco and John Blocker gave all three of us a passing grade. We were really surprised. Around the chuck wagon supper that evening, Rosita came up to me and whispered, "Meet me in the hayloft about midnight and I'll have a surprise for you."

She did too. It was quite an evening, or should I say *night*? I went back to my bed after four a.m. I sure hoped she didn't get in trouble. I'll tell you about it sometime.

About a week later, Chaco told me to come to his office. He had a letter from Captain Maxey. I opened it and read,

> To the rangers at Cardenas Ranch:
>
> Just wanted you to be aware that Karl Zimmer was spotted by a sheriff at Three Rivers. If you follow the Leona River south, it runs into the Frio River, which meanders southeast until it empties into a lake in Cherokee Canyon. On the other end of the lake, the Atascosa River comes from the north. Just south of this lake is the Nueces River; hence the name Three Rivers. The sheriff told me that a bartender found out from one of the men with Zimmer, who had too much to drink, that Zimmer and a former ranger were headed into the Nueces Strip. This is probably the ranger who sneaked him out of jail in Austin. His name is Al Holton. I want you to stay where you are and let your beard grow if you can. At least don't shave for a while and try to grow a handlebar mustache. In about three months I'll have some orders for you unless something changes before that time.

I showed the letter to Chaco. He read slowly and then said, "Looks like our friend is heading for the wild country. Let me explain what is there."

He told me about some of the towns south of the Nueces, which gave the name to this area. It was a hiding place for all kinds of riffraff, such as soldiers who had deserted the army, robbers of all kinds who were wanted for their work, murderers, women abusers, and anyone else who was hiding from the law. There were a few large ranches in the area and several smaller ones. The largest was the King Ranch that covered most of the South Texas area clear to the valley of the Rio Grande.

"I have an uncle who owns a big rancho south of Laredo between Ygnacio and Zapata. His name is Carlos Cardenas. He and my father were brothers. If you need help, he will send vaqueros, or you can go to his ranch and stay. I've already written him about you concerning the Zimmer trouble. He wanted to come here to help, but I told him to stay at home for now."

"Chaco, you are a real friend. I hope someday to be able to repay you," I said.

"Señor Buck, I am so deep in debt to you, I'll never get out, no matter what all I do for you."

We left it at that. I asked him how I could see Rosita without all the chaperones, and he said it would be next to impossible, but with a smile on his face he said he would figure out a way.

The next day we continued the reata contest. I really liked the idea of a long reata and, in my spare time, was working on a cowhide to cut some strands for a seventy-foot-long one. Tab and Toady were also working on some long ones. My time to run for a steer was next, and I gave it all my attention. I knew Rosita was there watching. I finally got the reata swinging up and over my head, and we were nearing the steer. I cut loose with my throw and could not have been luckier. It sailed around both horns, and my horse settled back for the jolt. We won, and the steer flipped back and over on his side. Two vaqueros grabbed him before he could move, and my horse kept the reata tight until they gave the signal to let them have some slack so the steer could be turned loose.

I knew that was only one catch, but I acted as though I had done it many times before. All the vaqueros and Tab and Toady cheered me and shook my hand. I would remember this one for a long time. I'd be lucky to catch another one, but I did on the fourth run. Tab caught one on his fifth run, and Toady had one on his fourth.

My fifth run was not 'til in the morning, along with two vaqueros who had caught two steers each. The three of us were tied at two apiece. It would sure be hard to duplicate my last two throws. Rosita had seen both my catches but left before we finished each day. I was sure disappointed. I wanted her to tell me in person how good I had done. No such luck.

I had worked late trying to finish my new reata. It measured sixty-six feet in length. Tab helped me to stretch it tight, then he and Toady and I spent a little time putting lard on it. When we got that done, we stretched it again and it measured about sixty-eight feet. It would be fine if I could make it work. I was sure going to try my best, because the two vaqueros were the best on Chaco's ranch. It would be no sin to get beat by them. They had been using a reata for several years, and I was just a newcomer.

After breakfast, John Blocker rode up in a carriage with his wife and two sons. Chaco introduced them to us. It would be a good day. I could tell. What I did not know was who it would be a good day for. Anyway, I hoped Rosita was there to watch me rope my last steer. I had great hopes. As we went to the arena, both the other vaqueros came over and shook my hand and wished me good luck. I returned the good luck to them. The more I was around the Mexican crew, the better I liked them. I decided if I ever had a ranch, most of my hands would be Mexican if I could get some to work for me.

Rosita walked up to me and wished me luck, then she walked to the stands with her chaperone. I wondered if Chaco had figured a way for me to see her alone, or if he was if he was just passing time with me. Tab and Toady wished me luck, and I told them I sure hoped they caught a steer today. The vaquero Ricardo was first to rope, and he drew a big steer with horns spread over six feet. He had the steer within reach and sailed a perfect throw and set the horse. The steer was down and on its side as two men grabbed it. Ricardo let the slack into the reata, and they released the steer. Looked like I had my work cut out for me.

Tab came up for his fifth run and made short work in catching a small steer that had horns about seven feet wide. He sure made it look easy. That gave him two for his roping. Toady missed his, and I sure gave him a hard time. I knew he'd get even with me, so I wanted to get the jump on him. The other vaquero was named Pancho, and he got a big steer with horn spread of about eight feet. It proved to be a fast runner, and Pancho's caballo had a hard time catching up. Thanks to a long seventy-foot reata, Pancho got close enough to throw it. It circled around one horn and was about to drop off the other one when the steer dropped his head and turned right under the loop. Pancho set his horse for a perfect catch. Cheers went up all around.

It finally came my time, and my stomach was turning over just like it did when I was with Julie Benton or when Mom died. I dedicated this run to both of them in hopes that it would bring me better luck. The steer I drew was a big one too. He had at least eight-foot horns. It would take all my skill and a lot of luck. I was riding my best roping horse.

The steer took off at an angle to the left and sped off. My horse slipped but recovered and quickly ate up the difference. I had him in my grasp, so I began raising the big loop up and over my head. Just as I was about to throw it, that crazy steer put on his brakes. The rope sailed past him a little ways, but my horse bumped the steer and shoved it forward enough that one horn was caught as the three of us went down in a tangle. I didn't know it, but several vaqueros came running out to help.

When the dust settled, I was tied to the horse and the steer. We were all down, and the steer was bawling and the horse squealing. All I could do was moan. Chaco and one other vaquero had their Arkansas toothpicks out and begin cutting my new reata. I didn't care; I just wanted out of there. When the reata was cut through in a number of places, the horse got up and scrambled away. The steer got up on three legs and crippled away, looking back to see what had happened.

I did not know if I could get up until Rosita came up and grabbed my hand. She said, "Buck, are you hurt?" Anyone with good sense could tell I wasn't in too good a shape, but my pride was hurt bad.

"I think I'm okay. Let me get up on one knee and see if I can stand up." Luis took my arm and helped me up. I made it fine, but I had to stand there awhile to get over the dizzy spell. Rosita had my hand by now and was squeezing the life out of it, but I didn't let on. John Blocker walked up and saw that I was going to be fine. I grinned at him, and for some reason I stuck my finger at him and said, "You big rascal, this is all your fault."

We all had a big laugh at that and then I congratulated the two winners. All the hands were glad no one was seriously injured. The next day was the time Chaco had set for the biggest feast ever. Everyone for miles around was invited, and the Blockers stayed the night. I spent most of the night with pencil and paper in hand. Toady and Tab thought I was writing to my brother, but I had already done that. I didn't tell them what I was doing.

The feast started about two p.m. I was really hungry by then. Rosita came up and asked me to sit with her. I was really surprised, but she said Chaco had arranged it for me. I thanked her for the invitation and stammered out how proud I would be to sit by her. Tab and Toady could fend for themselves this one time. The Blockers sat across from us, and Chaco sat at the head of the long table. I guess there must've been over two hundred people there. The food was fantastic. Plenty of it, too.

After the meal, Chaco got up and announced the winners. Each of the two winners got a fifty-dollar bonus, which brought a great cheer from all the guests. That was a lot of money. I had tied with Tab and three others with two steers each. We each got a new sixty-five-foot reata for our efforts. I really needed the new one to replace the one I had lost.

After the announcements of the winners, I asked Chaco if I could say something. He told me to go ahead.

"Today I want to express my appreciation for the way we have been treated here. Toady and Tab and I have made some lifelong friends, and I hope you all feel the same toward us. Last night I wrote a poem I would like to share with you."

I took the paper out and began to read:

The Big Loop

It was a long time ago that I got myself crippled up this away,
And I aim to tell ye it were not fun at all, but I'm sure gonna say;
You see, folks, it was on the Rancho de Viboro when I was a young
Cowboy, about twenty years old I guess, since me and Tab J

Decided we was going to rope us a real Longhorn steer we saw
That had a horn spread of more than eight foot at least to the tips;
I don't reck'n that's a record because we heard the Old Timers
Tell of some that spread more'n twelve foot, wider'n some ships.

I'm about to get ahead of myself, so I'll back up a bit if I'm allowed,
And since this is my story, I just reck'n I've got a right to do that;
We was in South Texas and had made a good friend of a vaquero
Named Chaco, who was a ropin' rascal or I'll eat my old hat.

Now, this Chaco made him a reata, which us Texicans called a
Lariat, and it was more'n seventy foot long made of three strands
Of cowhide, which was wove tightly into a smooth rope-like thing
After it was oiled and stretched tight with a pair of strong hands.

That thing was some kind of heavy, and it took some doing to get
It up over yore hat and headin' in a circle so as to make a throw;
Chaco worked several days with us before he ever let us mount a
Horse, and then the horse had to get used to that big loop, I know.

In addition to all of that, there was a feller name of John Blocker
Who invented a bigger loop fer them Longhorns and it was great;
That thing, when opened up right, would circle around a set of them
Horns over ten foot wide, and it was adopted in pert near ever' state.

It was known far and wide as a "John Blocker Loop," and I did my best
To learn how to throw it by workin' at it most every day fer a year;
Tab also worked hard, and Chaco was there all the time, and I'll tell a
Man, we owed him plenty fer all the teachin' and his good cheer.

Well, me and Tab and Chaco rode out one day into the wild brush
To see if we could find us one of them real Longhorn steers or cow;
After about an hour, Chaco hollered out they was one to our left
Near an open place, so we lit in after it, and me and Tab made a vow:

Whoever it was that was closest got the first shot at the critter, and
I mean the first throw at this big old steer was what we'd both need;
Since I was the closest, Chaco yelled at me to loosen up my reata;
So, after about fifteen minutes we had him goin' close to full speed.

I finally got my rope goin' in a big circle beside my horse and then
Gradually started it up and over the top of my head best I could;
I was gainin' on the steer, and just as I let go of my rope, that dumb
Steer threw on his brakes and if they's a God, help me if He would.

I'll slow it down and let you get a clear picture of what was about to
Happen as my horse was tryin' to jump that crazy steer at his feet;
He nearly made it and would have except my rope had cleared the
Right horn as we all tumbled in a pile that no one would call neat.

When the dust finally settled, Chaco and Tab had jumped off their
Mounts and were trying to untangle the mess including all three
Of us, the horse, the steer, and me; it seems the big John Blocker
Loop had settled around my left leg, with the horses back leg, see.

In addition, the left front leg of the steer was tied up with the other
Hind leg of the horse and then was wrapped around my waist;
With every kick of either hind leg it was crushing my desire to live,
Finally, Chaco got his long Arkansas toothpick out in great haste

And proceeded to make short work of seventy foot of my new rope;
That was the least of my worries at that time; the steer was done in,
My horse was about crippled, and I could do nothing but groan as
They made a travois to haul me back home where it all had begin.

I managed to keep my job after the boss had a big laugh and saw
None of us had been killed, even though I sometimes wished I had;
You see, it ain't no fun bein' camp cook, or Coosie, as I was called,
And John Blocker, I wished he'd of never been borned, by Dad.

Writ by Buck Bradley, a lucky cowboy

Boy, the cheering that went on would almost bust your eardrums. Nobody knew that I could write a poem. I even surprised myself, but Rosita stole the show when she ran up and grabbed me and planted a kiss right on my mouth. I was stunned. Chaco just grinned. Sure glad he was on my side. John Blocker shook my hand and asked me to make him a copy. Rosita said she would make several copies so anyone who wanted one could have it.

Several wanted to know where I got all the ideas for the poem. They knew the roping was an accident, and I made it out to be a lot worse than it turned out to be. I bragged about storing up things to use in my writing. Later that evening Rosita had two horses saddled and waiting for us. Looked real interesting to me. It was too.

I told the Blockers how happy I was to get to know them. He invited us to come to his ranch and stay awhile. We all agreed to do that. Several others came by to wish us well. It was a fun day, even though I did not win.

Rosita and I rode slowly toward one of the small lakes just south of the headquarters place. It took us about thirty minutes to get there, but I didn't care. When we got to the lake, there was a grove of oak trees but not the big kind. I think they called them post oaks. There was plenty of grass, and when we unsaddled I noticed a blanket spread out in one spot beneath one of the bigger trees. A picnic basket was on the blanket. Rosita grinned and took my hand and led me to the blanket, where we sat for a few minutes. I better stop here and maybe I'll tell you what else happened. Maybe I won't either.

It was quite late that night when we rode back to the barn. Two vaqueros grinned at me and took our horses. Rosita went to the house, and I went to the bunk house. Several hoots and whistles greeted me as I entered. Several had sat up playing cards and had just gone to bed when I walked in. They wanted to know what happened to me, but I pretended ignorance and they groaned and grunted.

"Yeah, we know, you lousy gringo. Can't tell the truth without gettin' in trouble. Wait 'til morning when we tell Chaco. Yore head will roll."

Morning came and went, but Chaco never showed up. We wondered where he was. Later that day we found out he had ridden over to the town of Pearsall to get a message from Billy Towson. He gave it to me when he got back. It was from Captain Maxey. I read it hurriedly and then I read it again. Slowly. The message was sort of brief, but Captain Maxey wanted the three of us to leave immediately and go the little town of Stockdale just forty or fifty miles southeast of San Antone. Chaco knew where it was—about seventy to seventy-five miles northeast of the ranch across some good ranchland. He gave us the names of some ranchers who would welcome us.

The next day we were ready to ride out. Chaco wanted us to leave three or four horses each and take only one spare along with us. The women fixed us a sack each of food for two days' travel. We said our good-byes and rode out. I sure hated to leave a certain lady behind and vowed to return as soon as possible. At least I had to come back after a horse or two, I said. Rosita hit me on the shoulder.

The telegram mentioned the name of the Cabbott Army. When I told Tab and Toady about it, Toady got a faraway look in his eyes. He knew that name as the ones who had killed all his family and friends south of Austin. I really felt for him but said nothing. When he could talk about it, he would. There was a ranger living in Stockdale that we were to see when we got there. He was a longtime peace officer and had been a ranger for five years. His name was Paul Howton.

Ranger Howton had a small office in the corner of a lawyer's office. The lawyer went by the name of Joseph H. Jones. He wanted us to call him Joey, which made him sound like a kid, but we did. Paul Howton was out but was due back soon. We made ourselves at home. I read a paper from Austin, which talked about the dry weather all around.

Joey wanted to know where I knew Paul from, but I let on as how I couldn't rightly remember. Until I was sure of Joey Jones, I wanted to keep myself kinda closed off. Never could tell when it might prove smart. Tab found an old magazine with a lot of pictures in it. He showed some of them to Toady, and several times they laughed out loud at them. I had no idea what was so funny until they showed me one. It was a cartoon of a caveman and a big fire-eating dragon. The caveman had the dragon by the tail, and he was slinging it around his head like a slingshot. The caveman was about four foot tall and skinny and the dragon was larger than our buffalo. That's what made it so funny.

A big man came into the office and looked at us.

"You men lookin' fer me?" he asked.

"We are if yore name is Howton," I said.

"It is. How kin I hep you?"

I took the letter from my pocket and handed it to him. He opened and read it. He handed it back and said, "Meet me at the livery stable around the corner. I'll be there in ten minutes." We walked out.

As we got our horses, Tab said, "Looks like he didn't want Joey to know who we are."

We rode around the corner and went into the stable. It had barely enough room for all of us, so we went back out on the street and waited. When Ranger Howton rode up, he smiled real big and got down. He held out a big hand and said, "Real glad you boys come. I didn't want Joey to hear what we're doin', so I told you to meet me here. He is married to a German girl. Seems nice enough, but I don't really trust her."

He motioned for us to follow him, and he led us to a small café where we got a cup of coffee and a slice of apple pie. When we finished the pie, he told us about some of the problems he was having in his neck of the woods. Seems the Cabbott Army had stolen several ranches in the area and killed or ran off the owners of three of the places. He needed some help in watching for them, so he had Captain Maxey notify us.

For the next hour we went over plans for the next few days. Tab was to stay with Ranger Howton, and me and Toady were to ride south about twenty miles and circle around to the west and come north along the San Antonio River until we met Rangers Paul and Tab. They were to ride north of Stockdale and circle to the west and meet us around the little town of La Vernia.

It took us all day to ride the twenty miles. We were in no hurry but sure wanted to look at all the possible places to hold a large group of riders and horses. We didn't see any logical places, so the night was spent with us not lighting a fire. We had cold jerky and water. The next day we started west toward the San Antonio River. As we approached the town of Floresville, we were met by three cowhands who ordered us to stop. They asked who we were. I responded with a greeting to them and asked directions to the next town that had a sheriff's office.

The front-riding poke asked again who we were and what we wanted with a sheriff. My answer was, "Cowpoke, we are from the state of Texas where people don't stick their nose out by askin' questions all the time. That way, their nose won't git cut off so quick."

He answered me with, "I'm from the same state, and I'll ask anybody a question I git ready. Now, who are you and what you want with a sheriff?"

I had been watching for any movement of his hand toward a gun, and he didn't make a move that way. I thought he might be a mite bit overconfident. I quickly drew my colt and pointed it at his chest.

"Now, sir, may I ask you again, where is the nearest town with a sheriff?"

He looked right into my pistol barrel and smiled as he replied, "Why, it's jist over the next hill about a mile. Be glad to show you the way."

I assured him we needed no escort, and they moved out of our path, so we moved on. They followed us all the way but stayed a ways behind.

We rode into the town and found the sheriff's office by the courthouse. We tied our horses and went inside. The sheriff greeted us with a frown.

"What kin I do fer ya?"

At least he was cordial, so I introduced myself as Corporal Buck Bradley and Toady as Private Toady Tallman.

"We are Texas Rangers and need yore help."

Toady gave me a funny look but said nothing.

The sheriff told us his name was Roger Wells and said, "Never knew a ranger to ask a sheriff fer help but glad you did. What kind of help you need?"

I replied, "We heard there was a military group around that goes by the name Cabbott Army. Are you familiar with that bunch?"

"Sure am. Everybody around knows them. They stole two ranches around here last year, but I got no proof. The owner's never been seen, and Cabbott came up with a bill of sale on the places. Kinda hard to press charges without knowing the facts. I can't git onto the places with so many guards at the gates."

"Reck'n I could git in his army if I volunteered and also Toady? That might give us an answer."

"Likely to be dangerous, but may be worth a try. Don't go there with new clothes or boots on or good guns or stuff. The man to see, if he is on one of these places, is a new man around here. Goes by the name of Zimmer. German, I guess."

Toady looked at me, and I winked at him. We said nothing about a Zimmer. It could be the Karl Zimmer who caused all the trouble with Chaco. Sure hoped to meet the man and find out. We thanked the sheriff after he gave us directions to the two ranches. We told him we'd keep him posted on any developments. We rode down the street and saw a sign that read "Telegraph Office" and pulled up. I went in and wrote a message to the Tuffy Bar and Café in Austin. He read it over and charged me fifty cents. After he sent it, he wadded the paper, but I asked for it back. He smoothed it out some and gave it to me.

When I got to the horses and Toady and I went out north on the main road, I showed the message to Toady. He read it out loud, "Mr. Tuffy, I have found the perfect ranch you have been looking for since last March. The price is right, and I'll meet you or your men in the next day or two on the San Antonio River about one mile west of Floresville. Bring plenty of money for a quick sale. Buck."

Toady asked me to explain again the secret code worked out by the ranger captain. I did.

"The message to Tuffy Bar and Café is the code for the telegraph office in Austin to alert the ranger office. The perfect ranch is for Karl Zimmer, and the location on the San Antonio River is the place to bring plenty of money, or men."

Toady shook his head and said, "I'll never understand your language."

"Sure you will, given enough time. Just keep tryin' and it'll be there," I assured him.

We rode north and east to get to the place on the San Antonio River. When we got there no one else was there, so we took our saddles off to rest the horses but kept the bridles on in case we needed to hurry. We heard horses coming from the west and saw three men coming across the river at a shallow place. It was Ranger Captain Maxey and two other rangers I had met when we caught Karl Zimmer. Their names were Tim Maxwell and Tommy Tucker.

They greeted us with a big smile and shook hands as though we were longtime friends.

"Howdy do, Ranger Buck and Ranger Toady. Shore glad to see you boys. These here are Ranger Maxwell and Ranger Tucker, but until later we are Burl, Tim, and Tommy, and you boys are Toady and Buck. Okay?"

"Sure sounds good to me, how 'bout you, Toady?"

"Fine with me," Toady replied.

"Now tell us what is goin' on 'round here, Buck."

I told 'em about meetin' Sheriff Wells and then showed the two maps to 'em.

Rangers Paul and Tab would be near La Vernia, and I showed 'em the place on the map marked by Sheriff Wells, only Sheriff Wells did not know we had the marked-up map. We had studied it and decided to locate a meetin' place after we left his office.

"I've been told by Ranger Paul that Sheriff Wells is a

dependable man and will side with us," Burl said. That sure made us feel better.

We made camp and cooked a little bacon to go with a can of red beans we opened. Toady had the coffee made in short order. It tasted good to all of us. We unrolled our blankets and bedded down for a few hours' sleep. I was ready fer it too. I slept like a log until about four a.m.. and woke up and put the coffee on. Some of the others woke up to the good smell and got up. We had a breakfast of jerky and coffee and headed north to La Vernia. It was about twelve miles to our meeting place. On the way, Ranger Maxey told us to separate and get behind some shrubbery until a rider came even with us. Ranger Maxey rode out and confronted the rider.

"Stop right there, Corporal Dancer. I want to talk to you," Burl said.

"Who are you and why talk to me? I ain't no corporal, and my name ain't Dancer."

"Just answer my question and you'll find out who we are and why we want to talk to you." By this time all of us had the man surrounded. He realized then that he had no chance to escape alive, so he began to get nervous.

"Now, Corporal Dancer, where is yore leader, Cabbott? Tell us now and escape a necktie party."

"Don't know no Cabbott. Let me go," he said.

"Ranger Toady, git yore rope and git it ready. Buck, find us a big tree with a strong limb. This feller's neck needs strechin' and soon."

Toady had already started makin' a hangman's knot on one end. I spotted a large oak about one hundred yards north, so we moved that direction. The Cabbott man was sweatin' up a storm.

Ranger Maxey went over and got the rope from Toady and put it around the man's neck, pulled it tight, and motioned

Toady to come closer. Toady got right in his face and in his wildest Indian voice screamed at him. The man cringed and started crying. Toady started in on him.

"You heap big man on river when kill all my people. Where all bravo now, big man? Want me cut yore privates off and feed 'em you?"

"Don't let 'im do this to me. I'll tell all I know. 'Sides that, I weren't in on the killin' he's talkin' 'bout."

By this time the man was lookin' death in the eye and he knew it. He begged Ranger Maxey for leniency if he confessed. Captain Maxey told him to confess first and then he would decide if the information was worth anything. He looked at each of us, as if begging would do any good. He began to cry some more and said he would tell us where their camp was.

Ranger Maxey loosened the rope some so the young man could relax a bit. He told us the camp was east of La Vernia and about twelve miles north and was on the south side of the Guadalupe River. That would be about fifteen or twenty miles from where we were.

"How old are you, Corporal?" Ranger Maxey asked.

"I'm fifteen."

"Kinda young fer an army man, ain't ye?"

He said he was not a regular army man but ran errands for General Cabbott.

"Where do you live, Sonny boy?"

He lived south of La Vernia about two miles on a farm. His mother and sister were all that were in the family, and he was working to help pay his own way. The farm had only pigs and chickens and a garden, so his mother and sister could do all that work easy enough.

"If we turn ye loose, will ye ride on home and fergit that Cabbott bunch?"

His answer did not surprise us. He swore he'd never see the Cabbott Army again if we'd turn him loose. Ranger Maxey told him he'd hang him high if he went back on his word. The young man thanked us all, and with tears in his eyes he waved good-bye as he left us.

"Shore hope thet youngster ain't lyin' to us."

We all nodded and said we did too. We decided to ride on toward the Guadalupe River and scout out the Cabbott Army. As we neared the camp it was almost night, and there was only one small fire burning. Two men were squatting near the fire.

We had met Tab and Ranger Paul, so that gave us a force of about twelve, which was enough to put some hurt on a larger group. Ranger Paul told me to join him and we would approach the two men at the fire.

"Hello, the camp!" Ranger Paul shouted. "Smelled yore coffee and could shore 'nuff use some."

One of the men put his hand on his rifle and replied, "Come on in if'n yore friendly."

We walked our horses slowly into the area, being careful not to place our hands in the area of our pistols.

"Where ye headin' this time of day?" one of them asked.

Ranger Paul replied, "Been down to La Vernia lookin' fer a ridin' job. Work's kinda scarce, and we missed a meal or two."

"Know thet feelin' fer shore. Been there myself a time or two. We got some bread and cold beans left over. Dig in if'n ye'd like."

"Right neighborly of y'all," I said.

They pointed us to a plate and cup, and we dished up a small helping of beans along with bread and poured a cup of coffee.

"Know of any work around these parts?" Ranger Paul asked.

"Heard of only one place over near Gonzales. Feller named Zimmer was lookin' fer some hands on his spread last month. May be all hired up by now. He's three miles south of there on this same river. Might check it out."

We assured him we would. They told us to camp nearby if we wanted, but we told them we'd ride on that direction a ways. As we got about two hundred yards away, I turned south and rode to find our group. They were waiting, and I told them about what the men had said. We rode on around and joined Ranger Paul.

"That camp was sure a big one fer only two men," Captain Maxey said.

"Sure was. It had several large tents and about a dozen two-man tents," I replied. "Cabbott must be on a trip somewhere."

Ranger Paul Howton told them about a man named Zimmer who had a ranch near Gonzales. We all talked it over and decided three of us would check it out. Since he would recognize Tab and Toady too easy, I took two other rangers with me the next morning to ride to the ranch. The others would ride back to the Cabbott camp to inquire about Cabbott.

Chapter 18

Rangers Bode Cowden and Tif Newly and I rode up to the gate leading up to Zimmer's ranch house. We had been given directions by a family in a wagon going into Gonzales. Our plans were for Bode to ask for riding jobs. I sure hoped Karl Zimmer did not know who I was. We hitched our horses and walked up to the door. Bode knocked and a puncher answered and opened it. When Bode pointed to us, he said all three of us needed work.

He looked us over and wanted to know where we had worked before. Each of us named a different ranch we knew about. He motioned us to come in and the boss would talk more with us. He led us into another room, and a man was seated behind a big desk with his back toward us. Two other men entered from another room. Each carried a rifle.

The man at the desk turned around and looked at us. He zeroed his eyes on me and said, "Well, if it ain't my old friend

Ranger Buck. Glad to see you. These men here will gladly take yore guns, so be kind enough to carefully lift them out and hand them over."

We had sure walked blind into this trouble. We carefully let them have the pistols. Zimmer would extract some revenge for the hanging of his younger brother. He let us know that in a very short time.

"Don't know how stupid you rangers think I am, but looks like I finally get to have my say. What are you doing here, anyway?"

Ranger Howton told him we were looking for work, and Zimmer smiled.

"Ranger pay too small fer you to live on? Why do ye think I have any work fer the likes of you?"

We told him he had the guns so do what he had to do. He did. He separated us to different rooms by having two armed men take each of us to other places. The room I went to had a small window high up and a bunk bed with a chair. That was all, and I guessed the others had similar rooms. My door was locked from the outside. It was about three hours later I heard a pistol shot and men shouting. Later I was told that Ranger Bode had tried to escape and was shot down. I doubted that was true. I mean about the escape part, not the shooting of the ranger.

After a short time, I was taken from my room and into the first room where we went to see Karl Zimmer. He was seated behind his desk, and Tif Newly was tied to a chair nearby. They tied me to another chair, but we could not see each other directly.

Karl Zimmer asked me, "Ranger Buck, how do you like bein' a ranger? They treat you like you want to be treated?"

I didn't know what he was after, so I asked him how he liked the ranching business.

"You answer me, boy, and don't git smart. That other ranger, Bode something or other, got smart and tried to escape. He never made it. You might git the same, see? I been wantin' to hang a ranger ever since my little innocent brother was hung by you all."

"Why don't you start with me and let Ranger Tif go home. He's got a wife and baby."

"So did my brother, but none of you even asked him, did ye?"

"Don't know what all was asked. But he was guilty of killin' and needed hangin', so he got it."

"Don't ye think some rangers need hanging? They been killin' too."

"Only in the line of duty," I replied.

Zimmer made a motion to one of his men, and he shot Tif in the shoulder. I figured I'd be next, but he motioned again and another shot was fired into Tif's other shoulder. He was bleeding all around now and was about to pass out. Then Zimmer motioned again and one of his men shot Tif in the foot. Tif passed out.

"How ye doin', Ranger Buck? Ready to stop a bullet or two, or had ye druther stretch yore neck?"

I had no answer for that. I really guessed it made no difference. I'd be dead, whichever he chose for me.

Zimmer motioned one of his men, and he came to me and hit me on the head with his rifle butt. When I finally came to my senses, I was lying on the grass under a large oak tree. I tried to raise up but was tied securely with a lariat.

The man who hit me came over and told me that Ranger Tif had gone to his reward. He asked me if I was ready to join him. I told him where he could go and he hit me again. This time it was not hard enough to knock me out, even though I wished it had been. My head was throbbing, and with two knots on it, it must've been three sizes larger. Wonder what made me think of that. Guess folks about to pass on think all kinds of crazy things.

The man was joined by several more, including Karl Zimmer. He was talking to me.

"Well, Mr. Ranger Buck Bradley, how does it feel to be on the short end of the stick? Did ye really think ye could git the best of me? Have ye made up yore mind to be hung or shot to pieces?"

"Suit yoreself. You seem to enjoy all of the ways they are to see people die."

Shots rang out from behind the house and around both sides of the barn. I could not see what all was happening, but several of Zimmer's men were down, and Karl Zimmer was holding his gut like it was falling out. The other men raised their hands and hollered out, "Don't shoot! We give up!"

Several rangers, including Toady and Tab, came running up to see if I was alive. When I assured them I was not hurt, they grinned as they saw the knots on my head.

"Good thing they hit yore head, Buck. Any other place might have been fatal," Tab said. Toady agreed.

The rangers had searched all the barns, bunk house, and the main house. Both rangers' bodies were found. They had been murdered just as I would have been if not for the good thinking of Ranger Captain Maxey. I sure owed him a big debt of gratitude I could never repay. When I expressed that idea to him, he said, "Yes, you can, Buck. You can carry the bad news to the families of the two good men we lost today."

The look on my face must've told the whole story of what it meant to be a loyal ranger. It was not a desired but necessary part of our duty, which we had all agreed to.

The good part of today was Karl Zimmer. He had slowly

died as he bled internally. He moaned a lot before he finally breathed his last. I said a silent prayer of thanksgiving that he was gone. Looked like our troubles with him were over, and the ranches he had stolen would be returned to the original owners if they could be found.

It took me several days to get over the "big head," and I never wanted that to happen again. We returned to Austin to hear plans being made to find the Cabbott Army. That would be a big job, but a needed one to bring about the end of one more crazy fanatic. Several rangers agreed to come to Austin next month, which was only six days away. We bade others good-bye for now.

Tab and Toady had quit teasing me about the big head and told me what they found on their trip. It was not much, but every little bit of information was a piece of the larger puzzle of peace in Texas. As we rode toward Austin, my mind wandered all the way back to my old home in Arkansas and about my mom, dad, and Toby. I also found time to think about a pretty girl there, and I wondered how she was and if I'd ever get to see her again. I vowed soon as we got the Cabbott thing under control, I'd go back and see them all and visit Mom's resting place.

The next few days passed fast. We filled each day with target practice, planning for the Cabbott trip, and picking our horses for the trip. Our rifles and pistols were cleaned each day after target practice, and we could take each one apart blindfolded and put them back right.

"Men, the word we have now is that Cabbott has moved on down the Guadalupe somewhere between Cuero and Victoria. We have two men down there now tryin' to locate the nearest place for us to go. We should hear from them by Saturday. If so, if any of you are churchgoers, I suggest that you go and be ready to move out by daylight Monday."

I sure did appreciate the attitude of Ranger Captain Maxey. I had not been to a worship of any kind in a long time. It got me to thinking about home and the preacher and his daughter again. I was beginning to really miss her. In case you've forgotten, her name was Julie Benton. I had to remind myself about her. I didn't ever want to forget her. I asked around Austin, and nobody knew about a church known back home as the Church of Christ. That surprised me some, as Brother Benton sounded like it was a well-known church. Maybe I would run across one somewhere.

We moved out early Monday. There were over twenty of us. We rode straight south of Austin and came to the Guadalupe. Here, the captain divided us into two groups; one was to take the east side and the other the west, and one group was to stay about two miles behind the other. I was in the first group on the east side along with Toady. Tab was in the other one. Our leader was a man known as Buck Broadway. We shared first handles, and we hit it off real good. He was raised up near the Red River also. It was near the town of Gainesville, Sivells Bend, he called it.

By this time I got to know all the men in my group. Four of them had helped Chaco secure his ranch against the Zimmer brothers. Two more had been in on the capture and killing of Karl Zimmer. We had a lot in common and talked a good deal at night with each other. These eleven rangers were well worth the saying of "good to ride the river with." They told me that meant that men like that were worth their salt, or they were good men in a tight to have around you. Anyway, I sure felt good about being with this bunch. I'm sure Tab felt the same about his group.

We camped about two miles from Cuero after the river made a sharp bend to the east, which put us just south of the little town. Two rangers were selected to ride into town and visit a bar if they had one. It was their job to listen for any talk about Cabbott. They came back with plenty.

"All right, men, here's what we know. Cabbott has only about thirty men in his army, and over half of them are new recruits. They are just south of us about eight miles. The river makes a sharp bend west for about a mile, then turns south for about three miles, then goes back east for three-fourths of a mile. The area inside this place is where they are. They are on the east side of the river. There is a little store just east of them, and it is called Thomaston, probably after the owner of the place. Any questions?" Captain Maxey asked.

"Just one, sir. Does the other group of rangers know all this?" I asked.

He replied, "They do now. I sent Ranger Ivey there an hour ago. Early tomorrow, we will go about two at a time, about twenty minutes apart, and head south. When we get near their camp, we will be on the east side, so we will come onto them first. The others will be slower due to the river turning like it does. Sergeant Buck Broadway will be our lead man, along with Corporal Buck Bradley. They will select the other groups of two who will follow. If possible, one of you can ride to the Thomaston store and see what is there. He may be in cahoots with Cabbott, so be alert."

I was chosen to ride to the store. I got there just before noon and went inside. He had a few cans of peaches, tomatoes, and beans. I paid for a can of peaches and went outside and cut the top off and drank the juice. It tasted good. I then slid one of the peach halves out and cut it in two pieces, which I ate. Before I could get another piece out of the can, two men and a boy about fourteen years old rode up and dismounted. They looked me over closely, and one stayed outside the store while the other man and boy went in.

The man who stayed outside never took his eyes off me. I

guess he was afraid I'd steal their horses. I continued to eat my peaches, then threw the empty can into a pile of nearby cans. Seems others had eaten here before. The other two came out carrying a few cans of something, probably peaches or tomatoes.

The man who came out with the boy asked me if I had a knife to open their cans. I told him I'd be glad to open them. They handed me three cans, which I opened. One of them asked me what I was doing there, and I replied, "Lookin' fer work."

The older man wanted to know what kind of work, and I told him I would like almost any kind if it paid.

"Ain't no payin' work 'round here, Sonny. Best move on elsewheres."

"My name is Jeff, it ain't Sonny, and I got no desire to leave jist yet."

"Well now, Sonny, supposin' you tell me why you ain't ready to leave," he said.

"Waitin' fer somebody to meet me. He told me to come here and wait fer him. Name of Cabbott," I said.

They looked at each other and back at me and the boy said, "Mr. Jeff, them Cabbott people is bad. You don't want to mix up with them."

"Hush up, boy. You let me do the talkin' or I'll skin yore hide."

The boy kinda skulked off like he'd been slapped on his head. The man who had waited outside all the time said, "Sir, if you want a real job, they sure are hard to come by 'round here, but I may have a chore or two you kin help me with. Don't pay much, but you kin stay in the barn on some straw, and Maw feeds good."

"Sounds good enough to me. Reck'n I could work fer a day or two. Where's yore place?"

"Foller this trail south about four miles to a great big dead oak. Turn east about a half a mile and my shack is there on the creek. Can't miss it. Name's Chaney, Joe Chaney. Come with me or come tomorrow."

I decided to go in the morning. As soon as they left the store, I got one more can of peaches and lit out for the ranger camp. I needed some advice from Sergeant Broadway, so I went to see him as soon as I found their camp. I spent about an hour with him and told of the Chaney invitation.

Broadway said, "Why don't you go there a few days and work. Maybe you can find more information for us that way. We'll kinda hang back until Monday of next week, so try to let us know."

I agreed and rode back toward the store. I decided to spend the balance of the short night about a mile from the Chaney place. Early in the morning I built me a small fire, warmed some coffee and some jerky, and finished the last can of peaches. It was quite a breakfast for the road.

Joe Chaney was in his corral trying to saddle a horse that he had not ridden in over six months. I smiled at him and greeted him warmly.

"Mornin', Jeff. Shore glad you could come. I'll let ye help me with this blasted gelding."

"If you'll hand me the halter or if you have a hackamore, I'd druther use it," I said.

"Got a hackamore in thet shed."

I went to the small shed and found an old rope he called a hackamore. It would do.

"Now, Joe, if you'll jist turn the horse loose and back away from him, I'll get him to where he can be rode in a little while." He looked at me to see if I's serious or funnin' him. When he saw I was serious, he dropped the halter and backed up to the gate and went out. After he left, I turned to see if the gate was closed. It was. I started the procedure Toady had taught us.

After about five minutes of talking quietly to the gelding, I gradually continued talking and walking slowly toward him. He would look at me, almost turn away, look at me again. By this time I had reached out slowly and touched his neck and began rubbing it easy-like, talking real quiet all the time. He was wondering when I'd swing the rope at him, but I had no such notion. After a few minutes, I put my arms around his neck, then backed away, and started to walk toward his side and rear. He looked around and started to turn to me. I spoke quietly and he stood still. I glanced at Joe, and he was staring at me with his mouth open.

By this time I had rubbed gently almost all the way around the gelding, and now, with the hackamore in my right hand, I reached up with my left and slid it under his neck, rubbing it gently. The gelding quivered some more. I gently raised the hackamore and put it over his neck. I now had both hands on it and was still talking to him. I slowly rubbed his jaws and worked the hackamore up and over both ears. Then I slowly took out the slack. Another look at Joe told me he did not believe what was happening.

I wrapped the end of the hackamore around the fence a couple of times and walked over to the saddle and blanket. I slowly showed the blanket to him, let him smell it, then rubbed his neck with it as I slowly worked it over his withers and onto his back. He acted like he wanted to buck and sling it off, but I continued talking and rubbing his neck. When he calmed some, I picked up the saddle, let him see it and smell it. His ears went back, so I talked him down to normal. I kept talking and rubbing his neck as I lifted the saddle and gently lowered it onto the blanket on his back.

He was startled by all this. Usually two or more cowboys

held his ears and another held a rope to keep him under control. The gelding was now standing without a quiver in his body, so I reached under and took the cinch strap and pulled it easily under his belly. I finally hooked it on to the proper strap of the saddle and started pulling it tight. He looked at me, but his ears stayed normal. I kept up the slow easy talk. I took the hackamore off the fence and started to walk away.

Joe couldn't believe it when the gelding slowly followed me. We walked all the way around the corral, and I walked over to where Joe was standing, the gelding just behind me.

"Slowly reach in and pet his neck, speaking real quiet."

He did, and the gelding, nervous at first, gradually let him rub his neck.

"All it takes is a little patience, and they become like real pets."

Joe said, "I've never in my life seen anything like this. You got to show Pa and Major Cabbott."

I didn't let on that I heard the Cabbott name.

"I'll shore be glad to, but first, let me mount up and see if'n he'll pitch me off."

I led him to the center of the corral, and taking the hackamore in my left hand, I lifted my left foot and placed it in the stirrup. Reaching with my right hand, I took hold of the saddle and put some weight in the stirrup. I quickly went back to ground with my weight and three or four more times I went up and down so he could get used to the weight. On the next move, I mounted him and settled my weight in the saddle. He was quivering, so I spoke again and dismounted. I played that game with him for about thirty minutes.

"Let's take the equipment off and do it again later today or tomorrow. I don't want him to get too excited about all this, so it's best to slow this part down. If he responds well in the morning, maybe I'll let ye try it."

He had not been able to saddle and ride the gelding for six months. Now he just might be able to. We went to the barn for a cloth to rub the gelding dry. Even though we didn't ride him, he was still sweating. Probably a nervous sweat, I told Joe.

"Rub me down too. I'm sweatin' myself," he joked.

We spent a few hours repairing fences around the house, barn, and small garden area. It felt good to be doing all that. Reminded me of home, except me and Toby was doing all the hard work. I thought of Toby and Pa and Julie, and every other thought was about Julie.

We spent another hour with the gelding before quitting for the day. This time, I let Joe do most of the talking, petting, rubbing, and putting the hackamore, blanket, and saddle on. That way, the gelding and him was "bonding," the experts called it. The experts was Toady's folks who taught him this method. The gelding was not too bad when Joe did most of the work. Joe did really good for the first time. I was proud of him and told him so. I was hoping for more information about Major Cabbott.

We worked the gelding twice a day for about four days, and then Joe told me we were to ride tomorrow to another place to work. He wouldn't tell me where, and I got kinda suspicious when he hung around me until late that night. I didn't have time to ride to the ranger camp.

Early the next morning, we ate a quick breakfast of eggs and bread and saddled up. We rode most of the morning south along the Guadalupe River. About noon I saw smoke rising and asked Joe about it.

"Is this where we're gonna work?"

He said it was, and we rode up to a formation between two large rocks. Two guards with rifles walked out to meet us.

"Hello, Joe. Who's yer friend?" one asked.

"This is Jeff, uh, I don't even know his last name."

"It's Lawson," I replied. The name did not seem to bother the two, so they told us to ride on in. About a half-mile farther we came to the main camp. There were only six tents, and one was larger than the other five. It was probably for Major Cabbott. We were told to dismount and hitch our horses to the rail where several others were tied.

We walked over to the main tent and started to go inside when one of the men came up with a pistol and stuck it in my face.

"Where ye thank yer goin', boy?"

I looked at him, and, without blinking, I said we were going in to see Major Cabbott.

"He ain't in there, Sonny. What ye want to see him about?"

Joe spoke up and told him about my great way of taming a horse so he could be rode in one hour. The man looked at me doubtful, then replied, "Can't nobody do anythin' that fast. Major Cabbott will want to see thet fer shore."

"Bring him out and I'll be glad to show all of you," I said.

"Jist be patient and he'll be along after a while. Meantime, hep yerselves to some vittles over there." He pointed to a big table near the big tent. We walked over there and filled a plate with beef, pork, chicken, and several kinds of vegetables and got a can of peaches. It sure looked like a feast for a king, and it was, except there was no king there.

We had to sleep on the ground with only a blanket from our pack and our saddle for a pillow. We were used to it. I was anyway. Couldn't tell about Joe, but he didn't complain out loud. The next morning at mealtime we were met by a little man about five foot two inches tall. He had a full beard and wore a funny-looking uniform. I guessed right when I figured this was the Cabbott leader. What kind of a leader was he?

He greeted me with a frown on his face. He looked like he had swallowed a dozen sour grapes or limes I'd heard about.

"What you want here, Sonny?"

"My name ain't Sonny. It's Jeff," I replied.

"Don't git sassy with me, Sonny. I'll call ye whatever I want and ye'll like it."

"I'll answer when you call me by my name, not some dumb thing you want."

"Sergeant Cully, lock this smart aleck in the barn."

"Ain't got no barn no more, sir. We ain't in the regular place no more."

"Then put a chain on 'im and bind his mouth. Can't stand no smart aleck that sasses me."

A man started for me, and I grabbed my pistol and aimed it right at the major.

I'd use it too, if they tried to force me. I knew the odds were not in my favor, but I didn't care for the major at all. His men started to spread out, and I knew they would have me if that happened, so I told the major he had five seconds to call them off. I started counting ...

"One ... two ... three ..."

"Stop, men. This kid's jist crazy 'nuff to kill me."

I kept the pistol pointed at the major.

"We's jist funnin', Jeff. I wanted to find out if'n ye had any guts. Can't use nobody thet ain't got guts."

I sure didn't believe him and didn't trust him at all. He must've wanted me to join up, but I did not want any part of his army. Joe spoke up and told him about me training his wild gelding.

He looked at me like I'd never been looked at before. His eyes got big as saucers.

"Ye think ye kin do thet?" he asked.

"I know I can but don't think I want to today." My pistol was still pointed his way.

He suggested we all sit down and have a cup of coffee. Sounded good to me, but I waited 'til the others had dismounted before I did. As I started to tie my horse, a shot rang out and I felt a hard slam on my back up high near my left shoulder. I fell but turned as I fell and aimed at the major. I fired my pistol twice before I blacked out.

Some time later I opened my eyes. At least I was not dead because I heard voices, voices I knew. Sergeant Buck Broadway said, "Welcome back, Buck. We hoped you'd wake up."

"What you doin' here, Sergeant?"

"We decided you had been here long enough and might need help. We was jist outside camp when you got shot. Yore two shots killed the major, and we took care of the rest. Joe there was the only one we saved out. He didn't take part in the battle."

I looked up and saw Joe. He had a big smile on his face.

"Jeff, I shore hate ye got shot. I yelled, but it was too late. One of them rats even shot at me, but he missed. I was real lucky."

I stuck my hand up and he took it. We had a nice visit about all that took place, and I introduced him to the men with Sergeant Broadway.

"You mean these are real Texas Rangers? I never seen one before."

"They sure are, Joe. So am I. We came over here to find the Cabbott Army. You kinda tipped me off the other day when you said you couldn't wait to tell yore paw and Major Cabbott about the horse-training session." I smiled and thanked him for what he did.

“How long was I out today?” I asked.

Joe answered, “Only about four hours today, but you was out all day yesterday and about six hours the day before.”

No wonder I felt so thirsty. Surprised I was not hungry though. Joe got a cool drink for me and handed me a biskit to go with it if I wanted it. I took it. I asked where we were and was told we were in the Cabbott headquarters tent. Sergeant Buck told me I had to stay a few days until I healed enough to ride back to Austin.

The next morning Captain Maxey rode in. He had our pay with him and told all of us thanks for the great job of putting away Major Cabbott. Toady was with him, and he had a big smile on his face that was mixed with tears. I really felt for him, but now he could put the slaughter of his tribe behind him. It would not be easy.

Tab and me were to meet with him after we ate our noon meal. It was sure great to see him, and all us rangers were proud men that day. Captain Maxey came over to my pallet and Tab came with him.

“Buck, you and Tab are due some time off, and it is my pleasure to order you to take it as soon as you can travel. I want you to go home and visit yore folks and friends. Take Tab to see his pa, then, return to Austin. Toady will go with Sergeant Broadway on a little job. After all three of you get back, I’ll have a major undertaking for you.”

Both of us took his hands and thanked him. We were ready to go north. He gave us a whole month to get there, visit, and come back. It took me four days to get up and around. Two more days, I was mounting a horse. I’d be ready to head north in another week after that. We had plenty of time, so we did not have to hurry or hurt my wound. Captain Maxey left with most of his men. Tab and two other rangers stayed to help me get up and around. I felt most gracious for their help.

Chapter 19

Tab and me said good-bye to our two ranger friends and started on the long journey to the Red River country. We each had two horses, so we could ride one and switch off every two or three hours. The weather was cooperative, which we appreciated. We headed northeast toward the Brazos River. We would probably cross it around Waco. Then we would cross the Trinity River southeast of the town of Dallas. My shoulder hurt a lot until we got north of the Sulfur River. We were back in familiar territory by this time. Tab could have ridden east to Jefferson, but he wanted us to stay together. We rode on toward the Red, where we would cross it north of Old Boston.

It had rained on us only twice on our trip north. When we got to the ferry that would take us across the Red, we were met by Drifty Thomas, who owned the ferry service. It had been over a year since I last saw him. He didn't know me but kept looking at Tab and me.

Finally he said, "Don't I know you boys?"

I replied, "You shore do, Mr. Thomas. I'm Jeff Bradley, and this is my best friend, Tab Alexander, who was taken from us by 'Slave Trader' Morton. We been gone over a year and this is my first trip home. Hope to see some folks and then go to Jefferson to see Tab's pa. We got him back from Morton too."

"Well now, seems you boys have been mighty busy this past year. Shore would like to hear about it sometime."

"I'd like nothin' better, sir. I'll try to find time to visit you soon. Right now I've got a young brother to see."

"Be his name Toby?"

"Yes, sir, it is. How'd ye know that?"

"He came through here t'other day and we visited a spell. Both you boys shore favor yore pa. I was sorry to hear about his tragic goin'. Seems that's all we hear 'bout these days. Makes a body wonder what all this world is comin' to."

"Thank ye, Mr. Thomas. Pa was a good man and didn't deserve to die like he did. I'll talk to Toby and try to see ye 'fore we leave here."

"I'd shore like that, Son."

We mounted our horses as soon as he tied the ferry. It was not very far to my home, about eighteen miles or so. I was ready to get there. So was Tab. We talked about the times we had as young boys.

"Rek'n thet girl of yores is still single, Buck?"

"She better be. I ain't heard from her in near a year. Then she ain't heard from me in that long either. Shore been missin' her."

"Guess that makes fer two of us. Been a while now. There

was a time or two I figured I'd never see these parts agin. Thanks to you, here I am, and powerful glad of it too."

He reached out his hand and I took it, and we rode that way near a mile. Friends are real people, and I was thankful for a real friend in Tab. I think he felt the same about me. It was dark when we reached my farm. We rode up to the front and a light was burning in the house. We tied our horses and walked to the door.

"Hello, the house!" I shouted. "We're hungry and need a place to sleep."

The door opened and Toby peered out; he jumped through the door and grabbed us both. Boy, was he excited. We went inside, and Mr. Traver's cousin, who had been staying on our place, came in and greeted us. He had been in the kitchen preparing supper, so he went back and added more to it. I could hardly wait to eat, and me and Tab washed up a bit out back at the pump. When we sat down to eat, Buddy Travers offered thanks for our food and also for our return to this home. I near cried because Ma and Pa was missing. Guess a body don't never get over that kind of loss. I didn't anyway.

It took us over three hours of talking full blast to cover the past year and what all had happened since we'd left home. I finally slowed down talking and asked Toby about his trip to the northwest with Pa. It took him over an hour to do it. He cried when he told about Pa. Me and Toby also shed tears. The rest of the story was real exciting, especially about the gold mine he had. I say had, because he sold it before he left. He had brought home over forty thousand dollars in his saddlebags. It was for a bigger farm for us. That would buy a big place and provide enough for horses, mules, plows, and everything we'd need. Toby was real proud.

"Pa had over seventy-five thousand dollars in his camp when the thieves killed him and stole all his money. We had worked real hard fer that much money. He was getting ready to sell his claim and come home. I had a hard time gittin' control of the claim. After all, I was jist a boy. William Story came back from his visits and heard about my problem, so he went to the mining authority and they investigated and gave me the claim."

"How come you to sell it, Toby?"

"Got homesick after Pa died. I wanted to come back and farm. Shore hope you'll join me, Jeff. You too, Tab. We'd shore make a good team."

"Me and Tab will have to think it over, brother. We got a good thing goin' with the Texas Rangers. But after Tab visits his pa over in Jefferson, he might could. Right, Tab?"

"Maybe so, but don't count on it. I shore like bein' a Texas Ranger. Ain't too many men of my color in the rangers, and my captain has me convinced of the influence I'd have if I make good."

"He'll do it too, or my name ain't Corporal Buck Bradley," I said.

Toby looked at us both and broke into a big grin.

"Y'all both amaze me."

"Now, Mr. Toby, tell me about my girl. Is she still as pretty as ever?"

"Don't rightly know if she is still pretty. Hain't seen her since I been back. Jist know she don't come to church anymore. Heard somebody say she up an' married 'bout six months ago."

I just about dropped my teeth with that remark. Boy, was I upset over hearing it. Well, can't say I was blaming her none. After all, I hadn't written her. I guess a girl has to look out for herself if they ain't no menfolk to look after 'em. Still, I was some upset, and both Toby and Tab knew it. They didn't say a thing, jist patted my shoulders. Supper didn't settle very good. My stomach turned over 'bout six times before morning. Tab wanted to get an early start in the morning, so we went to bed.

The next morning I felt like I had been stomped on by elephants, even though I'd never seen one. Jist heard they was big. Buddy Travers had a hot breakfast of bacon and eggs. Both came from our farm. I ate a little due to my stomach. Toby and Tab didn't have that problem and put away a good-sized meal.

It took us a few minutes to say our good-byes. I promised Toby that I'd shore consider his farming plan. Tab jist had watery eyes as he told Toby he'd know more after talking with his pa. Toby had offered a place for Tab's pa too.

We headed for the community of Ashdown. It was about twenty miles and would take us all day to get there. I wanted to find out firsthand about a certain pretty girl, and I could find out from her pa where she was. I was mad at myself for not writing her.

Well, we made it to their farm about dark. We had already eaten some biscuits and jerky, so we'd not bother them with a meal. The Bentons welcomed us like we belonged there.

"Both you boys have growed up to be big men now. We shore hated to hear about yore pa, Jeff. He was a good'n."

I thanked him and told him about Tab's pa over at the Morgan farm at Jefferson.

"That's where we're headin' now but wanted to come by and see Julie. Is she here?"

Brother Benton looked down with a frown on his face.

"'Fraid not, son. Julie left us fer a big travelin' whiskey peddler 'bout six months ago. We didn't know where she was 'til we got a letter from her. She was in Texas but would not tell where. At least she is alive and married the guy. His name is Vester Webster. That is about all we know, except we shore miss her and are heartsick she ran off like she did. Her letter was mailed from a town called Lakeview or Longview or somethin' like that. Me and Ma Benton was countin' on you takin' up with our Julie."

"I shore needed to write her some and stay in touch, but it seems I never found the time or place to do it. I guess it's my fault the way she did. Is there anything I kin do now?"

"Naw, guess she made her bed and will have to lie in it. Jist hope the feller treats her right. Her goin' away like she done shore ain't right with the Good Book I preach from. Maybe she'll come back some time soon."

"Me and Tab will sleep in yore barn tonight and leave early in the morning. I thank you fer the visit and wish I had written Julie."

Tab also said his thanks, and we went to the barn to tend our horses and bed down. It was near daylight when we left the barn and headed for the ferry south of Foreman. We spent the last part of the day and that night visiting with Drifty Thomas. It took us a while to tell about our experiences of the last year. He told us that the Morton feller was still coming through the area looking for slaves he could buy cheap or steal.

"Looks like you men will need to be on the lookout fer that crazy man," he said. We agreed. The next morning we headed south for Jefferson. A few days later we were riding toward the Morgan farm when we came upon a group of men in a fight. One of the men was bald and had a handlebar mustache. It was Slave Trader Morton. He and two other men were fighting with a black man, and we recognized him right off. It was Tab's pa, Moses Alexander. The other white man was Mr. Morgan.

We pulled our pistols out of saddlebags and waded in. Tab hollered to his pa and went to his aid. I headed my horse right into Mr. Morton and knocked him away. He was some upset with us and let out some words that ain't fit to hear. I got down off my horse and pointed my pistol at his gut.

"Back off," I said.

Morton looked at me and replied, "Git away and leave us be. We got bizness here and you ain't."

I had about enough from his mouth by this time, so I fired my pistol near his feet. He jumped away from where the shell hit.

"I'll git the law after you fer that," he said.

"Go right ahead. We are the law and will take you three men to Daingerfield to the sheriff and lock you up," I replied. Tab had his arm around his pa but still had his pistol pointed at the other two men.

"Mr. Morgan, I am shore glad to see you again. I'm Jeff Bradley."

"Thought so. Ye shore have growed up, son. What kin I do to help here?"

I handed him some leather strings from my saddlebag, and he got the idea real quick-like. As he started to get the men tied up, Morton grabbed at him. I just moved a little and swung my pistol and hit Morton a good lick upside his head. He fell like a sack of potatoes.

"Now you kin tie 'im up. Any of you other men want that, or will ye cooperate?"

They both grumbled but turned so Morgan could tie their hands behind their backs. Morton was tied hands and feet, so he could not move. I also put a tight bandana around his mouth. I did not want any of his sass.

"If we kin stay at yore place tonight, we'll haul these crooks to the law."

Mr. Morgan said, "We got us a new sheriff here and a jail to take 'em to. Sheriff's name is Webster. New to these parts but is a fine man. Why don't we take 'em there now? Ain't more'n three miles."

We took 'em, and I was some excited about this Sheriff Webster. Tab looked at me and grinned. The dirty dog. Webster was not there, so we got his helper to fix up the three men in a cell. Morton was put in a cell away from his men. He griped all the time, but I threatened to hit 'im agin and he shut up.

"Who do ye think ye are, lockin' up all of us?"

"If ye'll look close at us, I believe ye'll recognize the black men as two ye had stolen over near Ashdown last year, and I'm the one who found all of you down near Indianola and got them back."

He looked me over real good and said, "I know ye now. Ye gave me trouble in Foreman last year. I owe ye and will collect when I git out of here."

I told him I'd welcome his try. We left and went to the Morgan farm. I really wanted to see Milly. I was nearly over my embarrassment of her finding me neked last year.

Milly seemed real glad to see me. She kept looking at me and smiling like we belonged to each other. Shore didn't seem too bad a thought either. I smiled back at her every time. Mrs. Morgan and Milly cooked up some ham and eggs for all of us. It was really tasty.

"Miss Milly, don't reck'n I ever did proper thank ye fer helpin' me last year. Don't rightly know what might have happened if ye hadn't found me."

She smiled again and replied, "Jeff, or Buck, whichever you call yourself, I'm glad you were not hurt too bad. I'm also happy for your help in getting Mr. Alexander away from those men. We are so proud to have him work for us."

"Call me Buck, everybody does. I've grown to like that name. Both you women have really cooked up a good meal, and we thank ye fer it." Several amens were heard after my comment about the meal.

Mr. Morgan said, "Tomorrow morning Milly can show you around the farm. She knows all the pretty places fer young couples to walk and talk."

Milly turned red.

"Pa! Please!" she replied.

We went anyway, and she really showed me some neat places for picnics and such. We stayed out for about three hours, and I was about ready to see if I could hold her hand or maybe steal a kiss. She beat me to it. Boy, what a kiss. Nothin' like what Julie and me did. I liked it a lot and wanted another one, but she said it was time to go. We held hands all the way back nearly to her house.

When we were in the house and getting ready to eat the noon meal, Mrs. Morgan said, "Milly, why don't you tell Buck about the new girl you met several weeks ago. I'm sure he might even know her since they lived close to each other."

"Her name is Julie Webster, and she is from Ashdown. Her pa is the preacher for the Church of Christ there. Do you know her, Buck?"

"Sure do. Is she the wife of the sheriff here?"

Milly said she was.

"Our family and her family was good friends, but my folks are gone now and only Toby and me are left. Toby farms our place near Foreman."

"Sometime tell me about your folks, Buck. I wish I could've met them," Milly said.

I gave them a kind of brief history of my mom and dad. I had a hard time talking about them. Maybe sometime it would be easier, but right then it was hard.

Mr. Morgan and Tab wanted to go into town, and Moses said he needed some leather, so we all went. When we got to the jail we were surprised that Mr. Morton was not there. When I met the sheriff, he told me someone had posted bail for him and he got out. I asked what bail was and let on that I knew nothing about law things. He explained that it was a way for people to be out of jail but still under the law's supervision. If they ran away, the money put up for bail was kept by the law. He said it was one hundred dollars and felt sure Mr. Morton would stay around for his hearing, which would be scheduled later this week.

"I don't like it. That man stole Mr. Alexander as well as his son, Tab, here so he could sell them as slaves, which he did."

"I don't necessarily like it either, but I got to go by the law. Tell me yore name agin."

"It is Buck Bradley, and my friend here is Tab Alexander. The others ye know."

"Buck Bradley, huh? You ever live over near Foreman? Heard of a family over there by that name."

"That's my family, or was. Jist me and my brother left."

"I think you was the one chasin' after my wife, Julie. I know who ye are now, so don't be chasin' after her no more, hear me?"

"Don't reck'n I ever chased after her, but I'll leave it up to her if she wants to see me. Also don't like to be told I can't do nothin' I might want to."

He replied with a sneer, "Jist want ye to know, be careful around here."

I asked him who put up the money for Morton to get out, but he refused to give me a name. I could find out from a lawyer later, so I dropped it. We went out of the jail. I suspected that Morton promised him a bundle of money to let him out. The others agreed. We found Moses after he had bought his leather stuff and we left town. All of us were upset that Morton was on the loose. He was probably clear down into Texas by now. When we got back to the Morgan farm, Milly told us that someone had stolen her mare. She grew up with the mare and was really upset.

Tab and I quizzed her some and decided to track the mare and try to get it back. We found her tracks going southeast. We had already crossed Cypress Creek and came to another called Little Cypress Bayou. Both of them flowed into Caddo Lake. It was named after the Caddo Indians. The young Indian girl who had given me the buckskin suit was a Caddo.

The pines were plentiful and very tall in this area. About a mile farther, we both smelled smoke, so we dismounted and tied our horses. I took my rifle, and Tab already had his ready. We walked on the pine needles, careful not to step on any dead limbs or sticks that would crack like a rifle shot. We walked about twenty steps from each other, and I was slightly in the lead. I signaled Tab to come over to me.

"They're in a small clearing up there," I said as I pointed to the place. There was a wagon and a tent attached to it for shelter. Three horses were tied to the wagon tongue. We slowly made our way to the backside of the wagon when one of the horses began stomping and snorting. We held very still, but a man came out of the tent to look around. It was so dark in the tall pines that he had a hard time seeing anything. He went back inside the tent.

I sneaked closer and heard him telling Morton there was nothing out there.

Morton said, "Don't be tellin' me they ain't nuthin' out there. I know they is. Git yore skinny hide back out there and look at the horses. Don't want to lose any of 'em."

He got up grumbling and walked outside. By that time, Tab had made his way to the horses and hid. The man walked over to them, and Tab stuck his rifle in the man's back and whispered, "One sound and you are dead."

The man almost fell in fright. He made no sound. I went over and tied his hands behind him and put a rag tight around his mouth.

In a little bit another man came out to check on the first one.

"Bailley, you out here?"

Bailley could not answer.

The man yelled out, "Bailley, you okay?" He received no answer and started back to the tent. My pistol made a dent in his head as he walked hurriedly past me. When he fell, he must have fallen on an arm that was hurt because he groaned real loud as he hit the ground.

Morton came out and looked all around. I had left the second man where he had fallen, and Morton saw him and thought he was asleep. He let out a long loud string of cuss words that would curdle sweet milk. I was only a few feet from him and standing behind a large pine. Tab must have been on past him. When Morton got no response, he jumped up and grabbed his pistol and started firing it in a circle around the area. I waited for six shots, but there were only five. I stepped out and said, "Raise yore hands, Morton. You're under arrest."

Morton jumped and started to run for his horse when Tab stepped in front of him and said, "Stop right there, mister. You're under arrest."

Morton had another pistol in his belt that we didn't see, and he got it and started firing. Luckily, he missed Tab, but he got me. I went down, and as I fell, I heard him cussin' and saying, "You got me, you dirty Nigger. I should've killed you in South Texas."

Tab took aim and shot him in the chest. Morton was dead

when he hit the ground. Tab ran over to me and saw that I was breathing. He asked where I had been hit. I pointed to my head. Tab found where the bullet had grazed the area just above my left ear.

He said, "Lucky for you he hit you in the head. They ain't nuthin' up there to hurt."

We both laughed, but my head hurt too much, so I stopped. Tab had a rag and some salve and cleaned the area and treated it.

He fixed me a place to sleep if I could. The next morning he fixed coffee, and we had cold biskits with the coffee. I was glad to be able to eat anything. One inch over and Tab could have had my brains for lunch. He hooked two horses to the wagon and tied the other one, which was Milly's, and our two behind the wagon. He piled Morton's men in the wagon. They got no breakfast, and Tab told them they was lucky he didn't feed them a lead breakfast. He put Morton in the back of the wagon and covered him with a tarp. The tent he folded up and made me a pallet in the front just behind the seat. It took us about two hours to get to the Morgan farm.

Milly saw the wagon first and ran to hug her mare. When she got there she saw me and screamed. "Buck, are you alive? What happened? Where did you go? Who are these men?"

"Slow down," I said. "One question at a time."

By this time Milly's ma and pa were there. Mr. Morgan helped me up, and Tab helped the two men up. Milly was hangin' on my arm as we made it to the house. Mrs. Morgan had a bed made for me. It was in the house and not the tack room in the barn. After things settled down, Tab did most of the talking, and we filled them in on what all had happened. Tab seemed very glad that Morton would no longer bother the black people. He hid any bad feelings about killing Morton.

It was nearly a week before I could walk around easy. I could not put my hat on yet. The head was still swollen even though Mrs. Morgan had treated it two or three times a day, with Milly's help, of course. Tab and his pa worked around the barn and fences with Milly's pa. I just lay around until I got over being dizzy. I wanted to work some too, but they wouldn't let me. Finally, I got to go help Milly gather the eggs. What a chore for a Texas Ranger. Tab would really kid me in front of all his ranger friends when he got the opportunity.

I really got to see a lot of Milly. I don't mean that in the way she saw me the first time—naked in her barn, knocked out, and barely alive. I mean we got to spend a lot of time together. We had about a week before we had to leave for Austin. I got to explain a lot about the rangers, and we walked over her farm and finally got to ride horses. My head hurt some, but I rode anyway. Milly and me hit it off just fine. It got to the point where I was just about ready to try and kiss her.

We were in her favorite place on the farm in a heavy tree area near a small creek. She had a picnic ready and a blanket to spread on the grass. It reminded me of the times I went on picnics with Julie Benton. I wondered if I should tell Milly about those times. Anyway, Milly took my hands as we sat in the shade. She smiled at me and said, "Buck, do you think I'm bold?"

I didn't rightly know what to say, so I asked what she meant.

She said, "Buck Bradley, if you don't kiss me right now, I'm going to kiss you."We reached out for each other, and what a kiss. That went on for about an hour. What a time.

Finally, she said, "We've got to go back home now. I want you to know that I care for you a lot. Do you feel the same about me?"

I needed Ma to help find an answer, but she couldn't anymore. It was up to me.

"Milly, I really do like you and want to be with you more. I shore don't see how that is possible while I'm a ranger and traveling all over South Texas. You'll probably meet somebody and marry them just like Julie did."

"I wanted to ask you about her. She seems like a real sweet girl. Do you mind if we become good friends?"

"She needs a friend right now. I talked to her pa a few days before I got here, and he didn't know much about the man she married except that he was a bootlegger. Which reminds me, I need to go in and report to him all the facts about the killin' of Morton. He may not take kindly to me about that. He already warned me to stay away from Julie."

"Will you stay away from her?"

I didn't know what to say, so I did not answer right then. I guess she knew there was something about me and Julie, so she didn't say anymore. I told her I had a really good time and hoped we could do it again. She replied she did too, and, yes, we should go again. For some reason, it got kinda cool right then. I guess it's a girl thing. I didn't know what else.

We loaded the two men in the wagon provided by Milly's pa. We would leave it at the jail. It made a nice arrangement for us. Sure saved a long trip to the sheriff's office clear up to Daingerfield. We got the two into the jail and all locked up. Tab was visiting with two young black girls. He introduced me to them when I walked up. "Buck, these is my cousins. Here is Tabitha and that'n is Rachel."

"Well, I'm shore glad to meet some pretty kin of Tab. He ain't much to look at. Where y'all live?"

"Out'n the country near here. We only come in to see Tab. Ain't seed him in a while," Tabitha said. "We nearly got the same name."

"Yeah, I noticed that. Tab tell ye he got that slave trader?"

"Yessir, and we is very glad he ain't 'round no mo," Rachel said. "I ran ever time I seed 'im."

"Well, girls," Tab said, "we got to be goin' now. Tell yore mama I'll try to see her when I can."

"Bye, Tab and Mr. Buck. You come too."

We mounted our horses and rode slowly toward the Morgan farm. I wanted to see Milly before we headed south.

Chapter 20

By the time it took us to reach Austin, I was healed and rarin' to get back to rangerin' agin. Tab gave me a hard time most of the way. It had to do with my girl troubles. I acted like I was mad at 'im but was secretly glad he cared. I could not've had a better ridin' partner. We reached Austin about two weeks later and were glad to see so many good friends again.

I gave the report to Captain Maxey, and he congratulated both of us for the end of one Slave Trader Morton.

"You both will be up for citations of courage and bravery on this one."

That excited both of us, but I told Captain Maxey that Tab deserved all the credit. He assured me that we were partners, so I would share the spotlight with Tab. We received a great welcome from all our ranger group. What a treat to be working with such men.

"Buck, I'm goin' to send Tab over east of here to check out some reports of violence, and I want you to go on down to Chaco's ranch. We got a new report of more trouble there Get ready by day after tomorrow. Any questions from either of you?"

We had none, so we left and went to see about our gear to take on our next trip.

Tab pulled out early the next morning, and we didn't know when we might get back together. I left the next day for the Rattlesnake Ranch, eagerly awaiting a visit with a certain black-headed girl there. The grass was tall but dry most of the way. It had rained a lot but quit and was now turning into a full-fledged drought. I guess folks in the region were used to it, but I wasn't. It always rained plenty in Arkansas. Arkansas? I thought of Julie. Wondered how she is by now.

The trip to Chaco's rancho was uneventful. I wondered what kind of trouble he was having this time. I thought we had all that behind him, but I thought wrong. I had skirted around San Antone to the west and headed south to Pearsall. I got to the telegraph office just as Billy Towson was closing for the evening. We went to the café for some supper. What we ate was much better than the beef jerky I had earlier in the day. Billy told me there were no messages for me. I filled him in on much that Tab and me had done in the past few weeks.

"Sounds like you might jist keep on 'til you die of lead poison one of these days."

I assured him I had no such plans. I asked if he knew what the trouble was at Chaco's. He did and told me.

"Rosita was kidnapped or disappeared about a week ago. Chaco suspects she was kidnapped. Someone had seen a cousin of Karl Zimmer in the area. His name is Adolph Brightenkamp. He had grown up with Karl and Hermann up at Fredericksburg, but left there years ago to ranch out in the Paso del Norte country."

"Does Chaco have any idea where he might be now?"

"The sheriff of Del Rio reported that Adolph and a group of his cowboys came through there last week on the way west. They had some women, and one was a young Mexican with coal black hair. Probably Rosita. They caused no problems and rode away."

"Guess that means I'll ride to see Chaco tomorrow."

"Why not stay with me tonight? Got plenty of room."

That was the best offer I had, so I did. The next day I rode to the ranch and was met by several vaqueros. They were surprised but glad to see me. They filled me in on the way to the ranch house. Chaco had ridden north to check on some water gaps and cattle. He got back late that evening. He was surprised to see me.

"Welcome home, Señor Buck. I wish Rosita could be here too. Then all would be well, no?"

"It shore would, my friend. Tell me more. Billy Towson told me some of it."

"Mr. Towson knows about all that we do. There is one more word. Renaldo and Villareal just got back from Del Rio. The sheriff there told them about seeing Rosita with Adolph Brightenkamp. He saw nothing to be suspicious about. She was not tied or anything."

We talked late into the night. It took a while to tell him of the shooting of Slave Trader Morton and my near death and Jefferson. I didn't tell him about Milly Morgan. He told me that Toady had really made a lot of friends on the ranch. They all wanted to learn more about taming wild horses so easily. In the morning at breakfast I got to greet Toady and told him that Tab could rest easier now that the slave thief was permanently gone.

Two days later, Toady, Chaco, and four of his vaqueros and me saddled up for a trip to Paso del Norte. We each had two extra horses. We had three pack mules for our supplies. One of the vaqueros, Sancho, was in charge of the extra horses and mules. Guillermo was to be our cook. I forgot to mention we had a wagon pulled by two more mules. Guillermo drove the wagon. It carried extra saddles, bridles, rifles, pistols, and ammunition.

The trip was long and slow because of the wagon, but we might need all it contained. We stopped for a meal just north of Del Rio and went on our way. The way west to Alpine was hot and dry. We might need more water than we could carry. There were few known waterholes, and they were in the mountains around Alpine and Marfa. When we got near Marfa, we were treated to a great show of lights that no one knew how or why they happened. Every night we got to see them. When we left Marfa, a rancher told us to go west and follow the Rio. It made for better travel, and we'd have water. That's what we did.

When we got near Paso del Norte, we were told the name was now El Paso, which means "The Pass." Paso del Norte was for "The Pass to the North." Later the town would be called Magoffinsville, but that name would not survive. Maybe the post office people could not spell it, but they could spell El Paso.

El Paso was a desolate place, filled with mostly Mexicans along with a few whites. The town itself was built between the Rio Grande and a large string of mountains, the largest being Mount Franklin.

We inquired at the local sheriff's office about the ones we were following. He knew about the German rancher but had not seen or heard anything about a kidnapping lately. He would keep an eye out for us. The ranch we wanted was about ten miles northwest of town along the Rio in the "upper valley."

We rode up the river to Canutillo, a small village of mostly Mexican population. The owner of a little beer joint-café was named Joshua Vasquez. He was well-known as an honest man according to the sheriff of El Paso. We decided to eat there and went inside. It was crowded but comfortable. He served us some of the best steaks we had eaten in a long time. I was sure glad to make his acquaintance. So were the others.

Chaco found a rider who used to work for the German rancher. He told us the name of the ranch was the Rafter AB. The brand was the two letters of A and B with a kind of roof top over them. The AB was for Adolph Brightenkamp. It was a large rancho of more than ten sections that stretched clear over into New Mexico and north toward Las Cruces along the Rio. There was plenty of grazing land along the river, and Adolph had several thousand cows on the place. We saw them everywhere we rode.

Chaco and I sat up late the first night away from El Paso and planned our next move. We were fairly certain that our presence was known by the German rancher. Toady and I were to ride out first thing toward the ranch, and Chaco would follow with the others. They would wait 'til noon before riding after us. That way, it would appear that we were just two cowboys riding someplace in search of strays or perhaps a job.

We were stopped by three riders carrying rifles aimed at us.

"Who are you and where you ridin' today?"

Toady gave a sign that said he was a deaf mute and couldn't talk. They looked at him kinda funny and one said, "How 'bout you, Buster? Kin you talk?"

Well, I decided by the looks of the three men that I could and would talk, so I answered, "We're lookin' fer a ridin' job and were told you might be hiring, so here we are. Is one of you Mr. Brightenkamp?"

The youngest of the three appeared to be about my age, and he said, "Adolph is my uncle. How'd ye know about him?"

"I really didn't, but a man in El Paso in the saloon there told us about this ranch with a lot of cows. I think his name was Sam or Ham or somethin' like that."

"Reck'n that would be Sam Davidson at the Quarter Moon Saloon. He's all time sendin' bums this way fer a handout."

"We ain't lookin' fer no handout. We jist want a ridin' job. We kin ride or top out broncs or herd cattle or even build fence when we git hongry," I said.

"My uncle ain't hirin' today, so y'all jist turn around and head back where ye come from."

I looked at Toady, and he gave me a wink and reached for his pistol as I did the same. We caught the three by surprise and made them drop their pistols.

One of them said, "Ye dirty rats. Come up here to rob us and steal our cattle too. I'll git ye fer this."

I smiled at him and said, "Ye might be right, Jughead. Turn yore horse around and lead us to yore boss. We'll ask him real nice about a ridin' job."

The third man laughed as we referred to his partner as Jughead.

"Thet's a good title fer you, Bony. You remind me of a Jughead horse I had one time."

They led us about two miles upriver to a group of shacks. About the time we got there, several riders came out from some trees and surrounded us. They were well-armed with rifles and pistols.

The leader of the new arrivals said, "Who ye got here, Bony?"

"Jist a couple of riders say they want jobs with Adolph."

"Bony, you and Guenther take these two up to the ranch house while we rustle up Mr. Brightenkamp. He's back up the way with the brandin' crew."

With that, they rode off at a lope and we dismounted for a short walk up to the house. On the way, I caught a glimpse of a black-haired girl running from the outhouse to the back of the ranch house. It could have been Rosita. I glanced at Toady. He also had seen her.

In a few minutes several riders pulled up to the hitchin' post in front of the house. They dismounted and stomped up on the porch. A big-chested man of about fifty or so came into the room where we were.

"Bony tells me you men are lookin' fer ridin' work. We got nothin' fer ye, but ye kin eat on us then git out of here."

"We shore do thank ye fer lettin' us eat first. Reck'n we'll jist take ye up on thet offer," I said. Toady just smiled and nodded his head.

"What's wrong with him? Can't he even talk?"

I shook my head to say no to the question, and they did not question us anymore. They took us to the bunk house, and we washed up a bit and went to the kitchen to get some food.

Toady walked close and whispered, "I saw Rosita and she recognized us with a quick wave. How can we get her?"

I had no answer right then, so I smiled at him as we went for the food. There was plenty of it. Adolph believed in feeding his guests well. Later, we were seated around on the floor of the porch and talking with some of the ranch hands about the country north of here up toward Las Cruces. One of them told us the town name was "The Crosses," which accounted for the three crosses mounted on a hillside outside of town.

Adolph Brightenkamp had quizzed us thoroughly before we ate and was satisfied we were who we said we were. He did not question us as to who we had ridden with before coming to his ranch. After a bit, he came out on the porch and sat down between me and Toady. We looked at him and started to say something to him when all at once gunfire erupted up the road. Adolph jumped up and started across the porch to look. I just happened to stick my leg out, and he tripped on it and fell off the porch. I dove on top of him before he could recover.

I had my pistol sticking into his throat before he knew what happened. Toady was on his other side and had taken his pistol away from the holster. Adolph was not a happy camper. We watched as a group of riders came charging up toward the house. They looked at us and at Adolph. He gave them a sign of some kind and they quieted down. Among the riders was one I had recognized as one of Karl Zimmer's hands. He looked at me in a puzzled way but said nothing.

"Mr. Brightenkamp, we found a lot of people camping near our front gate along the Rio Bravo. What do we do with them?"

Adolph looked at him and said, "How do I know, stupid! Can't you tell what's going on here?"

The man looked at the pistol sticking up near Adolph's neck. His eyes got big as saucers. The man swallowed big and looked around. None of the men with him said anything.

After a bit, Adolph said, "Why don't we talk about this, sir?" He was indicating me.

"Sure thing, Mr. Brightenkamp. Jist have yore men leave their hardware here on the porch and they kin go to the barn or bunk house and wait while we talk."

They took off their belts and put them on the porch and headed to the bunk house.

"Don't try anything funny, men. I don't want to get a neck full of holes," he said.

They must've believed we might try it, so they left without so much as a bad word from any of them. Adolph relaxed when I removed the pistol. He wanted to know who we were or thought we were to come onto his property without his permission.

"Jist so ye know the truth, Adolph, Toady here and me are Texas Rangers, and we are here to arrest ye fer kidnappin' a lady from the Rattlesnake Ranch over near Pearsall. Her name is Rosita Cardenas, and we believe she is here on this ranch. Now, ye kin come with us while we search the place, or I'll tie ye up and look without ye."

"You men are crazy. I don't know anything about a lady from a ranch named after a rattlesnake or even a town called Pearsall. Let me loose or I'll call all my men."

"One or all, call them and ye'll never call any one anymore. I'm through foolin' with ye. Tell me where she is or I'll ..." I raised my pistol from the holster and acted as though I was ready to slug him on the head.

"Hold it! I'll have her brought out. Just don't get too careless with that iron."

"What are ye waitin' for? Get her out here."

He yelled out to a woman named Caroline to bring Rosita. She did, and Rosita came running to me and exclaimed, "Buck, it really is you. I've been so scared for two weeks now. They told me you were killed."

She had been crying and finally grabbed me around the neck and kissed me big right on the mouth. Toady just grinned and watched. What could I do?

I told her that Chaco and the others would be here before

too much longer. We got real lucky and captured Adolph before too much had happened. Adolph just kept frowning and shaking his head as though he would never get over letting two rangers capture him so easily.

Chaco and his crew did arrive shortly and couldn't believe what all they missed. He and I, along with Toady and two other vaqueros, had a private discussion. We agreed that Adolph had not harmed Rosita and would no longer be a threat to her or the Rancho de Viboro. They agreed not to prosecute Adolph as long as he stayed away from their ranch and caused no more trouble. I wanted to send a telegram to Captain Burl Maxey and see what he thought. We decided to take Adolph Brightenkamp with us to El Paso so I could send the message to Austin.

The next morning, a large contingent of riders, horses, and wagons headed for El Paso. It was noon before we arrived at the ranger office. We were greeted by a Corporal Snow, who was the only ranger in town. Two others had left the night before to go east toward Ysleta to investigate a large uprising of some kind there involving a group of Chinese laborers. They would not be back before the next day.

I sent the telegram to Captain Maxey and waited for the answer. It came about two hours later. He congratulated us on the job we did and wanted us to hold Adolph for further questioning. We took him to the local jail and had him put under close supervision at all times. In the meantime we went to a large hotel called the Plaza, which was on the square downtown. We each had a room and all had baths before meeting in the lobby for a short walk to a local eating place that was suggested.

Chaco and I walked with Rosita to the café. The food was excellent. The square where the hotel was located was tree-lined and was a beautiful shady area of a whole city block.

There was a large central area that was filled with water, and ducks were swimming around and large fish could be seen in the water. It was very nice. Rosita and I lingered for a time around the water area. She put her arms around my neck, pulled my head down, and kissed me again.

"That, dear Mr. Ranger Buck, is for getting me away from those men. When we get back to the rancho, I may have something better for you."

I could only imagine what she had in mind. By the way, I nearly forgot to mention that I kissed her back.

A telegram came for me the next morning. We had planned to leave by noon, but after getting the telegram, we ate together and I shared the news with all the group. Captain Maxey congratulated us and said he would "do it up right" when he saw us. Tab was to return to Austin by way of the Rattlesnake Ranch.

My assignment would take me to Brackettville, which was about thirty miles east of Del Rio. That would put me about seventy-five to eighty miles west by northwest of Chaco's ranch. I told them that I'd be able to handle that, provided that I could take off a few days here and there. I smiled at Rosita and received a big smile back. Yes, sir, things were getting better.

I went into Del Rio and found the General Store. It also had a restaurant and clothes. I needed a set of clothes from my head down, so I started looking at hats. There were several that I liked and chose one that had a dignified look to it. Several of the rangers had that kind. The clerk, who turned out to be the owner, helped to crease it. His name was Davidson and said he had two sons about my age. One was Bob, who ran a large sheep ranch in New Mexico, and the other son was Dave, who worked in the store. I ate with Dave.

Dave was well aware of problems along the border and helped me understand what the people in the area had to put up with. He kept referring to the Nueces Strip. I asked him about it.

"If you go west from here to Uvalde, you'll cross the Nueces near Uvalde. From there south along the river all the way to Cotulla and west across to Three Rivers, the Nueces turns southeast all the way down to the gulf. The closest town on the gulf is Corpus Christi."

I had never been that far down and told him about being on Chaco's ranch. He looked at me in surprise.

I asked him, "Why the puzzled look? Do you know Chaco?"

He replied that they sold many cattle and sheep to Chaco's family over the years and many ranch supplies.

"That is one of the best families in this whole area. How do you know him?"

It took me about an hour to explain some details of recent happenings.

"I thought it odd a few days ago when some cowboys came in the store and had a beautiful black-haired Mexican girl with them. She tried to pass a note to Dad, but one of them intercepted it. I bet that was Chaco's sister."

"It was and is. She has now been reunited with her family, thanks to a dedicated group of rangers. The man who kidnapped her is a cousin of the family I told you about who gave Chaco such a bad time."

We were about to head back to the store when two cowboys walked in. One was the spittin' image of Dave.

Dave said, "Hey, Bob and Joey, come over here and meet a new friend." He introduced us to both and gave Bob a brief synopsis of our conversation. Bob knew about Chaco's run-in with the Zimmer brothers. He also said, "We rode through

Langtry, and Judge Roy Bean fined Zimmers' cousin for carrying a pistol in town. He collected fifty dollars for each of five men in the group. Oh, in case you don't know about Judge Roy Bean, he is the self-appointed judge of Langtry and surrounding territory. If I were you, I'd steer clear of him. Heard he found a dead man in the alley behind a bar and the man had a pistol and forty dollars in a pocket. The judge fined him forty dollars for carrying a concealed weapon."

That brought a laugh from all of us.

We went back to their store where I finished buying the items needed. They included two shirts, some waisted overalls, a belt, socks, and a pair of boots. I also got three boxes of shells for my pistol and rifle. Dave showed me a new doeskin shirt like I had on. He wanted five dollars for it, so I got it. I went to the table near the back of the store, and Bob continued the talk of the Nueces Strip.

"There have been some terrible men come into the Strip over the years. When it gets too hot in their home area, they all seem to know about this Strip. It would be best if you stayed very alert while here, and don't trust nobody."

"Sounds like good advice. Do you know Bill Belcher over at Brackett? I'm to meet him in a couple of days. He's a rancher near there."

"We know him well. Good, honest man. Traded bulls with him several times. Give 'im our regards."

I promised I would. I paid the bill I owed them and thanked them for the meal and conversation. It was time I headed for Brackett, so I loaded up my packhorse and rode east. As I rode, I thought about Judge Bean. He had a large picture of an actress named Jersey Lil behind his bar. It was quite a picture if it was true. I decided I might stop in sometime if I was in the area. About thirty miles farther, I came upon some construction. It turned out to be a new Fort Clark, and

I didn't know why it was needed. Maybe Bill Belcher could tell me.

I rode up to his place about noon the next day. Bill and his crew were working cattle, so he told me to get down and cool off in the shade of a big oak tree. I did both. About an hour later he came over and told me to ride up to the house and we'd get a steak. He had an excellent cook. She'd been on the place for over thirty years, which turned out to be his age.

Bill was easy to talk with. He seemed to know all the history of the area, as he was raised on the place and did business from San Antone to Del Rio. He also cautioned me about the Strip. His ranch was joined to the Y-O Ranch, which was about six times as large as his and covered over six thousand acres. Chaco's place was only about seventy-five to eighty miles farther east and south a ways. Maybe I could sneak over and visit Rosita.

I explained to Bill about all the drugs that were coming into Texas, and he knew about it. Much of it was coming across at Eagle Pass in Texas and from Piedras Negras across the Rio.

He said, "Stay over a few days and we'll go down that way and you can check it out."

I agreed to stay, and the next day we rode south to a place northwest of Eagle Pass about thirteen miles. It was a small city of mostly adobe brick, cedar post, and grass. Name of Normandy. We rode in and stopped at a place that had a sign of food and rest. We partook of both. We also had a smithy look over our horses for signs of loose shoes.

"Buck, I got a letter from your captain about four months ago. His wife is my cousin. In his letter he told me some about you and what you have meant to the rangers. He was quite proud. So I'm glad to be of assistance and will be happy to give what help I can. That includes my ranch and all my employees."

That sure sounded good to me, and I told him so.

"Do you know the Davidson family in Del Rio?" I asked.

"Sure do. We have many business dealings together. Dave is a very good cattleman, and Bob is no slouch. We like to get together and rope calves whenever time allows. Do you rope?"

I had never thought about roping and told him I'd like to give it a try sometime. He promised to show me how and even provide a horse and lariat.

He said, "There's a rancher in Del Rio who taught all the Davidsons how to rope. His name is Jim Altizer, and if they had a world championship, he'd probably win it. Maybe you'll get to meet him while you're around this area. Now, tell me about this drug problem, as you call it."

We spent the afternoon discussing what little I knew, but the main thing was, the one's who were shipping drugs into Texas were getting rich and people were fighting to control who got to handle the supply.

"So, if we can identify the main suppliers, we might be able to cut off some of the drugs. The main one is marijuana, but some are very dangerous. Some may even be raised here on the border. That is what my main job is now. So, where do I start?"

"I'd suggest eating a good steak before we walk around and meet some of the people here."

"Bill, you're my kind of man. Which steak is best here?"

"Rib-eye if they got it."

They did, and we ate a big ten-ounce one with potatoes and glass of cold beer. I didn't really want it, but I drank it, and it was wet and cold and really set the steak and potatoes up real good. We finished the meal and walked around and met three people on the square. I made a mental note of each man and what he looked like and the business he ran. That might come in handy sometime. Bill introduced me as a rancher looking for a place around the area. They told us about one that sounded favorable about three miles north of Eagle Pass, which would be about seven or eight miles south of where we were. We decided to ride there in the morning and check it out. The owner had died of some strange disease, and the family had moved back to Tennessee, where they came from.

We located a man in Normandy who was handling the property, and he agreed to meet us for an early breakfast so we could get there and have time to look over the place. We met as soon as the café opened, which was six a.m. His name was Joseph Alladin, and no, he was not kinned to the lamp man. It took us a few hours to ride the eight miles to the place. I wanted to go slow so I could mark some of the area in my mind. It would prove profitable later.

When we got there, Mr. Alladin told us the place was supposed to be empty and no cattle would be there. He was wrong on both accounts. We were met at the gate by three vaqueros who were heavily armed and would not let us pass without a signed letter from the owner. Mr. Alladin proved very efficient in this area and conversed very well with one of the men in Spanish. We were told to ride on into Eagle Pass and ask in the bank for a Mr. Leon Valmoor. By the time we got to the bank, it was after noon, so we went to the stables located on the north side of town. We saw the bank sign about a block farther on. We got our horses fed and watered and stabled and walked down to the bank.

Leon Valmoor met us at the door of his bank. He was going next door for coffee and asked us to join him. He had already met Joe Alladin and greeted us in a friendly way. I wondered why Joseph Alladin did not say anything about knowing the banker. I filed that question for later. Leon Valmoor proved to be quite knowing about the area and tried to impress upon us that we had come to the right place for a spread. Well, I'd have to think on that, but I let him know how much I appreciated his help.

We agreed to meet early the next morning to see the ranch. When we got there, there were no cattle anywhere that we could see. I asked him and he had a ready answer. A neighbor rancher had been grazing the place until yesterday, and his short lease had run out. He had moved the cattle last night. I recalled one brand, a Lazy LV. It did not take me long to figure that out. The place was about five thousandacres and bordered the Rio for about one mile. It was covered with grass, and all along the river trees were in abundance. It would be a nice small ranch, maybe just right for me and Rosita.

The house was not in good shape, but the small bunk house and two barns were in good repair. So were the corrals. The windmill was pumping water into a trough. The water was cold and tasted good to me. There were three other windmills and four ponds on the place. I made a mental note of the location of each windmill and each pond. The river border was not easy to access, except for two places where a trail was well used and recently too. Tracks were very evident, but I made no mention of them, but Bill Belcher nodded and winked at one place where there were several horse tracks as evidenced by shod feet. We both would have a lot to talk about that night.

Bill asked Mr. Valmoor for a copy of a map of the place. He agreed to furnish one if I bought the place. I told him that my memory was not good enough and I needed a map before I would agree to look farther.

"Well, come to my office tomorrow afternoon and I'll have it."

I agreed, and we rode back into town for a steak and bed.

Our conversation that night was a long one. We both agreed that it had been a good move to come and see the ranch. It looked like the ideal place for anything from Mexico to cross into Texas. In fact, I was really impressed with the place but would probably be better off not settling in this part of Texas. I liked the north parts better. One reason was, it rained more in northeast Texas. There was usually plenty of grass available. That was reason enough.

Chapter 20

Bill Belcher and I continued looking for a small ranch. We found one I liked better than the one we saw the other day. It had easy access to the river and was a well-traveled trail. There were several ponds full of water. Along with a nice set of barns and pens, there was a large house with three large bedrooms, a kitchen, and a room for a couple who might be cook and maid. One larger bedroom had a desk and could be an office. The place had 1,800 acres and about one half-mile of riverfront. Good hay pastures were all along the river bottom. Pecan trees were in abundance along the river.

"This looks like what I've been wantin', Bill. What do you think?"

"Sure looks okay to me. Let's go into town and find out who owns it and what he wants for it."

We rode into town and found a man who knew about the

place. He sent us to a small café on the east edge of town. Carlos Abriago met us at the door and told us about the place and owner.

"Señor Alberto Noches is the owner. His wife died and he has gone back to Mexico. I aim to sell the place for him."

Before we could find out more, two riders came up. One was Toady; the other was a young man who looked familiar, but I couldn't place him.

Toady said, "Buck, we've got some bad news, but first, do you remember the young man we caught up near Slaughter Ranch? His name is Karl, and he is distant kin to Brightenkamp and brings us the news."

"That's who he is. I've forgotten his name. First, tell us the news."

Young Karl looked up at me with a nervous look on his face. He then spoke with a wild-eyed frown on his face.

"I am Karl Brightenkamp and am a distant cousin to the Albert Brightenkamp. About two days after you left him, he sent his men after Rosita. They arrived at the Cardenas Ranch after dark and snuck up to the house while a lot of celebrating was going on. Rosita was in the middle of the room, and the bad men started shooting through the windows."

"The shooting lasted only a few minutes, but during that time, six men were killed in the room. Mr. Chaco was wounded in the shoulder, and Rosita was killed."

"Wait jist a minute, Karl. How do you know about all this?" I asked.

"Some of the ones who escaped told us. I had stayed at the Zimmer place after you told me to get away."

"How many of the Brightenkamp crew were killed?" Toady asked.

"All but two, and there were twelve who were there dead," he said.

I just stood there with a stunned look on my face. In my mind I had already planned a life with Rosita. That was over now. I determined to visit Chaco as soon as possible. The others in the room knew about my feelings for her, and they each came over and took my hand or patted me on the shoulder. I left the room before I started crying like a baby.

I rode to the telegraph office in Bracketville by myself and sent word to Ranger Captain Burl Maxey, asking for time to visit Chaco. He responded within one hour. His telegram expressed sorrow and wanted me to come to Austin after the visit to Chaco. I ate a late meal that night and slept in a hayloft so I could be alone. The next morning I bade Bill Belcher good-bye and thanked him for doing for me the things that only good friends do for each other. I rode toward Chaco's place. It was about forty miles to Uvalde. Toady rode with Karl Zimmer back to Rattlesnake Ranch. After I got to Uvalde, I spent half a day resting my horses. One shoe was loose, and I had a smithy tighten it for me.

The smithy was a kind man even though he was heavily bearded and looked meaner than a rattlesnake. His name was Martin Melrose, and he knew about the troubles the Zimmers had caused. He was not a friend to them. I took him to eat at their little café across the street from his shop. He must've weighed in at three hundred pounds and was six foot five inches. He ate like it too. Nearly broke me with what he ate. He insisted I stay at his house for the night. I did.

Early the next morning I bade Martin Melrose good-bye after thanking him for his hospitality. We could sure use more men like him around. The ride to Chaco's place was uneventful, giving me more than enough time to think about Rosita and the others who had been killed. I didn't know what I would do now. The small ranch I had wanted was probably out of the picture now. So were a lot of other things I had thought about.

A couple of days later I rode up to the family burial plots about a quarter of a mile south of the main ranch house. I dismounted slowly. I looked at several headboards and finally saw the fresh mound of dirt that was probably where Rosita had been buried. There was no marker, but it had to be the one. Tears welled up, and I could not say anything for a long time. I just stared at the ground and cried. Later I rode up to the shack where the hands were already bedded down.

Luis came out when he heard me ride up. He was solemn and greeted me quietly as I dismounted.

"Welcome back, amigo. Chaco has gone to Pearsall and will be back tomorrow. He said if you came, wait for him."

I asked him for more detail of the attack, and he gave it to me as I munched on leftover steak and potatoes with gravy and bread. The other hands greeted me warmly and expressed regret that I had not been there a few days ago. I sorely regretted it.

Sleep was hard to come by, even though I was tired from the long days of riding. I imagined my horses were as tired. I had started to tend them, and two of the vaqueros took over for me. I never tried to stop them.

Chaco came riding in about the middle of the afternoon. He had with him a man we had never seen before named Em Taylor. He was a tall, well-built man with bright red hair, about my age, and was a Deputy United States Marshall from Pearsall. He had come with Chaco to get more information about the Brightenkamp family. I asked him where he was when we had the problem in Pearsall.

"I've just been moved to this area from the North Texas area around Sherman."

I replied how happy I was to meet him and welcomed him like I was the owner instead of Chaco.

"Chaco filled me in on you and how much you mean to this family and ranch. We need men like you in all branches of law enforcement. Jist wish I had my way and had more money to hire more like you."

This was turning into what my pa had called a "mutual admiration society," so I changed the subject and asked him what else he had been working on.

"Nothin' excitin', but I manage to earn my pay. Jist the trivial jobs are enough to keep a feller busy. Next week, you and me are headin' down to the Nueces country fer a look. We think that's the place where Brightenkamp is doing most of his raidin' of the ranches. Here's a telegram that came fer you in Pearsall the other day."

I took it and thanked him for bringing it to me. Saved me a trip over there. The message was from Captain Maxey and confirmed my going with Marshal Taylor. I folded it and put it in my pocket. I looked at Chaco, and he had a big grin on his face. I wondered why he wasn't sad-faced after losing Rosita.

He said, "Come on in the house, Buck. We need to go over some plans for this week."

"Sure," I said, still not understanding what was going on. The four of us went in as one of Chaco's vaqueros took our horses. Chaco led us into the huge room he called the living room. It had several big, comfortable chairs and two divans. There was a long table with ten chairs around it. There was one chair on each end with four down each side. We sat at one end, and Chaco took the end chair. He called for one of his servants to bring us some drinks and cakes. He still had that unusual smile on his face, making me wonder more what was going on. As the maid came back shortly with the fixings, I had to do a double-take as I looked at her. I looked up and again looked at her. She was the spittin' image of Rosita, maybe a cousin I didn't know about.

As the maid walked around the big table serving the others, I kept looking at her. I was to be the last one served if she continued on. That was okay with me, as I was enjoying looking at her. Finally, she came to my chair, placed the serving at my plate, then she set her tray down, smiled at me, and said, "Is something wrong, Señor Buck? Do you not remember Rosita?"

I jumped up and grabbed her to see if she was real. When she kissed me, I knew she was for real. Tears ran down my face and joined those on her face. I didn't know what was happening, but I was the happiest man alive to see and hold on to Rosita. I finally looked at Chaco for an explanation. He said later on that I would be given the information.

"Why don't you and Rosita go into the sitting room and get reacquainted?"

We wasted no time getting there. Rosita held me tightly around my waist until we took a seat after closing the door. We continued holding each other and crying our eyes out for some time.

"When the bad men raided our rancho, there were many bullets fired, and my dear friend, Daniella, who looks a lot like me, was the one who died. It is her grave in our cemetery. Chaco thought it best for me to stay in the house for several days, which led many to believe that I had been killed."

"That must've worked, 'cause I was told by two different people you had been killed in the raid. You don't know how happy this makes me," I said.

"Sí, Buck, I am also very happy now that you know the truth and are here with me."

We sat and talked late into the night until she finally told me it was time for bed. My room was in the back of the house, and she opened the door for me but stayed in the hallway as the door closed us apart. The next morning I awoke to sounds coming from the kitchen. The cook was busy with breakfast and banged a few pans together. I dressed and went into the kitchen where Toady, Em, and Chaco were seated at a table drinking coffee. They gave me a cup already poured but had not been saucered and blowed. It was still hot.

Chaco was telling them about the raid, so he backed up and repeated some of it for me, then, continued on. Seems this Brightenkamp had come to the area from up on the Red River near a town called Muenster. That's where Em first came across the name. The town was full of German families who had settled there some years ago about six or eight miles south of the Red. Em told us that Brightenkamp was no longer welcome there, as he was not a good man. He robbed neighbors and travelers alike.

"This man is the reason for me being down here, Buck. I had known him and a couple of his brothers back there. They are a tough bunch, and being hurt or killed doesn't seem to worry any of them," Em said.

Chaco knew the place near Eagle Pass when I told him about it. He wanted to buy it for me or loan me the money, but I told him no on both counts. Captain Maxey had already told me the state would supply the money for the place and for enough cattle to stock it. It would be a good cover for me. I wrote up a detailed account about the ranch, its needs, and Leon Valmoor. I still had questions about Mr. Alladin, but those could be asked later.

Chaco read what I had written, and we addressed the letter to Austin. One of the vaqueros would ride to Pearsall tomorrow to post it. In the meantime, I would ride with Em on his mission.

I told Rosita about the small ranch near Eagle Pass, and she seemed excited about it. I almost asked her to marry me but lost my nerve. Maybe after I got back from the trip with Em and bought the place ... Her kisses almost got my nerve back. Then, for no reason I could think of, I remembered another girl up near Jefferson that I liked. I sure was confused about women, but I was not tired of them.

Chapter 21

Em and I stayed for two more days with Chaco. At least Em stayed with him. I hung around Rosita as much as she would let me. I knew if we were to marry, it would be a match made in heaven. The rider who went to Pearsall came in late the second day and had another bit of news for me. It was a special letter to me from Captain Maxey. It had a letter of credit to the bank in Eagle Pass that I could use to purchase the ranch and about fifty to seventy-five mother cows. That was hard for me to realize. Chaco and Em joined Toady as they all congratulated me for the event. I had to tell Rosita, but Chaco told me she was already in bed and I could not see her until morning.

The first thing I did when I awoke was to shave and put on some tonic the barber in Pearsall gave me. It sure smelled like roses or violets to me. Rosita was in the kitchen bothering the cook. He was glad to see me.

"Get her out of here, Señor Buck. She keeps getting in my way."

With that message, I grabbed her arm and said, "Out you go, mi querida. You need to come to the stable and help get my saddle on so I can leave."

The look she gave me melted my nerves again. But she came with me and we got a saddle and bridle for my best horse. Em would have to do his own. We looked, and Em was riding from the stable and leading another horse. I would join him in a few minutes, but not until I told Rosita the good news about the ranch we would buy.

"We?" she asked.

"Yes, we, Rosita. You and me."

"But Buck, I can't just leave here and go to your ranch. You do not understand our customs. Chaco must first give his approval after you have given me your proposal. Then we must wait for a period of time, have a big party, and celebrate the marriage."

"That all sounds good to me, except for the waiting part. But I'll ask anyway. Rosita, will you marry me?"

"Sure I will, my Buck. But let me think on it until you come back from the place you and the marshal are going. In the meantime, as you gringos say, you may kiss me."

Boy, did I ever!

After breakfast, Em and I mounted up and rode toward the ranch and the town of Eagle Pass. Toady was to ride up to Austin for a visit with Captain Maxey.

We got to the ranch and rode around the place. The cattle were moved, and we saw no signs of any that were fresh. The house was fairly clean and livable, which pleased me a lot. Eagle Pass was to be my new home. Or should I say, the Buckhorn Ranch was to be my new home.

We took most of the next morning riding the fence line.

It needed some repair work but would have to wait until I got a wagon. Bill Belcher told me I could use his, so I rode to his place and he sent one of his hands with the wagon and some wire and tools. Bill was happy to hear from Em. They had known each other from an earlier time. Bill had told me some of the story about Em and the Mexican family he was acquainted with who were having problems very similar to that of Chaco.

After we started work on the fence, I asked Em about his girlfriend. He looked at me with a frown on his face. Seems he had no desire to talk about her, so I didn't push for a report. We took a noon break, and Em opened up some and told me about her.

"The last time I was there, I near got killed," he said. "Three of her vaqueros saved my hide, and boy, was I glad they came when they did. I could not see my way out of the spot I got myself into. I'll tell you about it later, but now I just want to think about how to solve your problem, then you can help me with mine."

We finished the fence repair the next day, and the Belcher hand left for his ranch. Em and I rode into Eagle Pass and spent a couple of hours at the local hardware store. It was owned by a friend of the Davidson brothers who had a bigger store at Del Rio. Bud Frazier was his name, and he also was a windmiller. We wanted him to come out soon and repair mine. I needed a new wheel and some sucker rods replaced. He promised to come out by the end of three days. Things were shaping up by the time he came and finished the repair work. Em and I were ready for some cattle.

Near the creek about a half-mile northwest of the house was a grove of tall trees. Em and I rode there with a couple of sharp axes and a crosscut saw. We selected two that stood about twenty-five feet tall and near straight up. We chopped and cut until both were down and then spent the next hour trimming the smaller limbs off. When that was done, we were ready for some water and food, but all we had was water and some jerky. It almost tasted good to us. We piled the smaller limbs together and put our reatas on the end of each large tree trunk. Our horses worked hard pulling them the half-mile home.

The next morning I bet Em he could not beat me in sign painting. The bet was the largest steak dinner in Eagle Pass. The sign was to be mounted on the two poles after we had them solid in the ground. It took us all day to dig the two holes about five or six feet deep. There was not much rock, so the digging was not too complicated, just hard and tiring. We decided it would be easier to paint and mount the sign before raising the poles. We went to work cutting two boards about twelve inches wide and ten feet long. The chiseling and smoothing took another two days. I was about ready to give up and hire someone to finish the job, but Em talked me out of it. We braced the two boards together along the back-side, so it appeared smooth on the front, and then painted the front white. It took three coats of paint, not including the coat on me and on Em.

After the paint dried we outlined the words “Buckhorn Ranch” in letters about fourteen inches high. Black paint filled in the letters. We spent another half-day digging two trenches starting at each hole and sloping back so we could slide the poles into their proper place. When the poles were pulled far enough toward the holes, we propped the sign up and, with ropes tight, let it slide into place. We tamped the poles as straight as our eyes could measure.

Em said, “Buck, we ought to go in business. This thing looks great.”

I agreed to one part, the one about it looking great. I had other plans than a life of building signs.

"Too hard," I said. But I did tell Em he won the steak and tomorrow we'd go to town and celebrate. We did! We also went to the bank to verify the letter of credit I had from Captain Maxey, even though his name was not on the letter. We did not want to blow my cover. The letter was from a big bank in Austin; that was more impressive.

I could taste the steak all the way to the Rattlesnake Ranch the next day. I wanted to see Chaco and not only buy the cows from him, but to ask for Rosita's hand while there. We came to the ranch property line from the south and were met by six vaqueros. One recognized me and let us through the gate.

"Welcome home, Señor Buck. It is so good to see you again. Who is the friend?"

I replied, "Good to see you too, amigo. This is Em Taylor, who is my partner in ranching at Eagle Pass. Em, shake hands with Luis Fernandez, best roper on this rancho."

They shook hands, and Luis introduced the other five. I had met all of them and tried to beat two in the horse-taming chore a few weeks past. I had told Em about that, and he wanted to try it when he had the time. The vaqueros split up and two rode with us to the main house.

Chaco was in a north pasture and would not be back until dark. That pleased me since I could now see Rosita. But she was with Chaco. We spent the time in the bunk house with a couple of injured vaqueros. They had both broken arms in falls after their horses stepped in holes in the ground. They were about healed but could do only menial tasks, like feeding and brushing horses. We helped them feed and then brushed a couple of horses for them.

Chaco came in with two other vaqueros, but Rosita was not with him. I was really disappointed, and he sensed it.

"Welcome, hermano, glad to see you and also Señor Em. Rosita had to stay with a family at one of the camps. The woman is very ill and has three little ones and needed help. Come in the house so we can visit, Buck."

Em said, "You go on in, Buck. I'll help these men with their horses."

Chaco wasted no time letting me know the latest details of the Brightenkamp situation. He had caused damage at three of the camps in the last month. Two more vaqueros lost their lives and five Brightenkamp men died.

"I really do not know where to place my men, Buck. He seems to know where he can come and go with the least problems."

"Guess me and Em could divide some places, like I could patrol the two south camps and Em could cover a west and north camp. Your men could cover the other three for a while. If Toady comes back, he could take an east camp, and maybe Captain Maxey could have Tab come down for a spell."

"That might work, Señor Buck. We could try it. Let's get our men together and go over the plan in more detail."

Right after the night meal, riders came charging in to the front and up to the tie rail. We went to see what was taking place.

A rider yelled out, "Señor Chaco! The north camp has been hit again. We have lost some more men and Rosita is hurt bad!"

We both ran to the barn, and as we got there, two men brought saddled horses out for Chaco and me. Several others were hauling their rigs to horses. We lit out at a fast pace to the camp. Chaco had given orders to several men to stay and guard the main place. Five others soon caught up and shared some biskits with us as we rode. Chaco had a deep frown across his face, so I remained quiet until he was ready to talk. It took us near an hour to get to the camp. It was quiet, and one vaquero came out to investigate.

"Señor Chaco, we were caught by surprise in the barn. They killed the Armondo brothers and Philipe Ruiz. We saw the man leading the attack, and it was the Señor Brightenkamp."

"What about the women, Lauro? Are they hurt?"

"Sí, Chaco. Three of our vaqueros loaded them in a wagon and are taking them to Señor Slaughter's rancho. They might get better care with all the women there."

"That is good, Lauro. What can we do now?"

"Pepe and Antonio followed them west. I don't know where they are now."

Chaco told me to get a fresh horse, and we headed west at a steady pace. We were nearing the river as the sun was coming up behind us. There was a bunch of clear tracks to see, so we continued on. We stopped at the river crossing and rested awhile and let the horses graze. After about thirty minutes we heard horses coming from the west. Pepe and Antonio rode up. Pepe had his arm tied up for support, and blood was dripping down his hand.

"Chaco, we found them. Two more of them died before we ran out of bullets. But the main man and three others went south about a mile west of the Rio. We can go after them."

Chico told them no for now. We attended Pepe's arm and stopped the blood loss. We went to the west camp where all was in order. Chaco explained what had happened. Several of the men were ready to ride after the outlaw bunch.

Pepe would stay there until his arm healed some. Chaco decided to ride to Slaughter Ranch. I sure wanted to ride along, but he wanted me to go south and try to get the German killers.

Seven of us rode south. Antonio rode up front with me. Em and three more vaqueros caught up before the first hour was gone. I was sure glad for the extra help. I told them all I knew, and Em was ready to go. I wished I could tell him that Rosita was alive, but I had no such information.

Chapter 22

We followed the trail they were leaving. It seemed as though they wanted us to catch up; the trail was so clear. We were about fifteen miles east of Bracketville when three cowboys rode up. They were from Bill Belcher's ranch. The one who brought the wagon to us was one of the riders.

After greetings were passed around, Big Joe, another of the three, said, "We were sent here by our boss. The captain at Fort Clark stopped a group of men yesterday who were headin' west and stopped in Brackett to eat. One of Bill Belcher's vaqueros overheard part of what was said. He told his boss, who then rode to Fort Clark with word that they were planning to stop west of Clark and wipe out the bunch that was doggin' 'em. That would be you men."

"Sycamore Creek is there and is about ten miles east of Del Rio. That is a likely place for the ambush," he said. "Captain

Angus Ashdown wants you to wait on our ranch. Chaco and his men will be comin' in a day or two to join in. Then we can plan our attack with the help of the fort. We should be able to provide up to one hundred fightin' men."

I quickly thanked him and had the men mount up for the ride to Belcher's place. Em and I rode side by side most of the way and stayed close that night. Em had said he would share a long story with me, so I told him I was ready for it.

"Just hang on, Buck. This may take a while."

He told me that he had been reared on a ranch between the Frio and the Sabinal Rivers. A big ranch southwest of there was owned by Fidencio Pinales. He had three sons and two daughters. Em had been a playmate of the younger son, Liberato, but had a more sincere desire to be close to the younger daughter, Lucinda. He had no chance to see her very often and was afraid she would marry before he made any headway.

"I was workin' on a ranch out west in the Pecos country around Fort Stockton when I hired on as sheriff of Balmorhea for three years. The U.S. Marshall at that time was Kip Mason, and he talked me into being a deputy for him, and here I am."

We talked for a couple of hours into the night and continued on the next morning. He really liked his job, danger and all. I had time to tell him about all the problems with the German brothers. He knew both and was glad they were gone. The Brightenkamp fellow was a different breed of cat. He apparently had few, if any, scruples and would steal or kill at any time or place. He had been the cause of the problems at the Pinales Ranch that Em was working on and wanted me to help with.

"I can get you an appointment as a Deputy U.S. Marshall, which has several advantages, one of which being you don't have to answer to the legislature in Austin, which changes every election year. The pay is about half again more than a Texas Ranger makes, and we ain't got no boundaries like you do."

"Keep talkin', Em. I like what I hear but don't want to make up my mind 'til I get this big problem solved and find out if Rosita and I can marry."

"I'll help with one but not the other."

We both had a big laugh.

Later that day Ranger Captain Maxey rode in earlier than we expected. He had with him three more rangers along with Chaco and five of his vaqueros. Another man was also there. It was Major Kip Mason, U.S. Marshall. He was Em's boss. Kip was a tall, blond, heavily muscled man. He was clean shaven and was quite a striking figure. Em greeted him warmly and introduced him around. Kip indicated he wanted a meeting of all the main leaders there.

"I am sure none of you have never worked with a U.S. Marshall before, so I want to be sure all of us understand who's in control. If Em and I were not here, Captain Maxey would be in charge, and after him would be the local officials, but we are here and that puts us in charge. However, Em and I are not as familiar with this case, so we defer to the rangers."

Several smiles could be seen around the group. There would be no problems with authority now.

Captain Maxey took over the planning, and he assigned me and Em to work as a team to divide all the men into about four groups. There would be about forty or more in each group. One man was assigned in each group to be in charge of weapons and ammo, another was to be in charge of horses, another for food and incidentals. One man was to be the special runner for his group to send news or to get help if needed. After all had been selected, Marshall Mason asked for all to assemble. He then did an unusual thing. He requested that all kneel down and remove their hats. Next, he led a long, beautiful prayer; he asked God for the safety of everyone and then final victory over the men we were about to fight. I was very impressed.

After we were dismissed to our groups, Marshall Mason came over to my group and asked me to join him for a few minutes. I felt real honored to be in the presence of this great servant.

"Corporal Bradley, are you related to or know the Bradleys at a little place in southeast Arkansas, I think they now call it Foreman?" I was caught by surprise but recovered enough to answer, "Yes, sir. My father, Tom Bradley, was raised there and was kin to the Warren Mason family from there."

"Then that makes us kinfolk, Corporal. Tell me about your folks."

I took a few minutes to explain about Mom's death, Dad's murder, and a few other details. He asked me questions that somebody who was not close kin would not know to ask. I told him about Toby and Mr. Story and how I happened to be a ranger. Then he asked about the Benton family, so I told him about Julie and me. He was a very good listener, and I promised myself I wanted to be more like that. We visited for about two hours, and I was really impressed by the man. Sometime I'll tell you all I could learn about him, but that's for later.

Marshall Mason took his group of riders all the way to Langtry, about fifty or sixty miles west of Del Rio. I took my group north up the Devil's River, where we would then head west toward the crossing of the Pecos. Em took his group to Comstock, then north about ten miles and then west to the Pecos. That left Chaco and Ranger Cantrell to head directly to the Pecos and come up from the south. According to the map drawn by Marshall Mason, we would hit from four points: north, east, south, and west of the crossing on the Pecos.

Plans had been made to attack at dawn on the fourth day, which would make it on Thursday. We said our good-byes and good luck and good hunting early on Monday as we ate together. It was a somber meeting. None of us knew who would not make it back home, but all of us had determined to do our best to be the one who made it back.

Chapter 23

When we were kids, we played a game where we divided up in two groups and played around our barn. What we were planning for this morning reminded me of this game when we called out, "Red Rover, Red Rover, let Toby come over!" Each time it was someone else whose name was called. Today, it was no game, but I wanted to shout out, "Let Brightenkamp come over!" I doubted that he'd come over. We would probably have to cross the Pecos to get him. If so, that's what we'd do. Looking west from where Em and I were to come into the action, we could not tell if it was time. We could not see anything back to the east where the sun would be coming up. We just hoped our timing was right.

Em's group was about five miles from me if the map was close to correct. I might be able to hear a rifle shot that far away since it was dark and quiet. I surely hoped so. I had my men spread out so no one could shoot into us and kill more than one per shot. I did not want it to be easy for our Mr. Brightenkamp. We rode carefully and as quiet as thirty horses could walk as we made our way southwest toward the Pecos. After about a mile, we each took a bandana and tied it around our horse's nose so they would not snort or neigh if they smelled another horse.

We rode carefully for another mile, and then shots started up south and west of us. We hurried our mounts and got our weapons ready. By then there was a steady racket of shots, rifle and pistol, mainly in the direction we were going. The firing increased as we guessed that other groups were closing in. They were. Suddenly, a group of about five horses with riders were coming toward us at a fast pace. Another group was chasing them. It was light enough to see clearly. I didn't know who was leading the first group but decided it had to be one of Brightenkamp's bunch. We rode out to stop them and fired at their horses. Two men fell as their horses were crippled.

Six of my vaqueros rode to the two men who went down; the rest of us rode after the ones trying to get away. We nearly had them surrounded, but three of my men were shot, or their horses were. The German group was down to three and heading north fast. Coming up behind them was Chaco and Ranger Cantrell. They rode in where I was and joined me. We raced on in hopes of catching them. One of them suddenly turned west and hurried that direction. Chaco and I followed and sent the others on north.

The horse we followed was a fast red stallion with a flowing mane. It seemed strange to me to notice something like that with my life hanging in the balance. Chaco motioned me to the right and he went to the left as we began to slowly catch up. Shots were being fired at us from the rider, but he was at a distinct disadvantage having to turn in his saddle and shoot back at us. That made me feel a little better, even though a bullet fired in any direction was still deadly if it hit the target.

We crossed a small creek that had no water in it. I guess it was really only a dry creek bed. Anyway, after crossing it we lost sight of the rider. Chaco came slowly in my direction, and as we rode slowly on north, Chaco noticed a difference in the hoof strides of the horse we were following. Maybe it was hurt or even shot in the leg. We didn't see any blood, but we separated a ways and rode on. We got about one hundred yards from a clump of trees ahead and shots were coming from them. We quickly looked for cover, and I found a low spot behind a cactus bed and dove off my horse into it. Lucky for me there were no rattlesnakes there, but there was not much cover either.

Chaco would have to look for his own cover, and I prayed he'd do so. After about five minutes, I looked up to see if there was any movement. There was. It happened to be a rifle slug headed my way. It caught me as I turned my head back north. Something like a heavy iron bar hit my head and lights went out.

I woke up after dark and didn't know where I was or what I was doing there. Maybe someone would light a lamp or something and clue me in. They did. It took me several minutes to fully wake up. When I woke up enough to realize what was going on, Chaco and Toady were in the room. They both welcomed me back from another world. It took both of them about an hour to explain what had happened.

Let me put this in my words so you can better understand. When Chaco and I dove for cover, he went to the left and I went to the right. When it quieted down some and no shots were being fired, I raised my head to look around. The turning of my head kept it from spilling my brains all over the place. Chaco kept up his watching for Brightenkamp and finally saw him make a break for his horse. Chaco beat him to the horse, and Brightenkamp saw he was losing; he grabbed his pistol and fired point-blank at Chaco. There were no bullets in his gun.

Chaco grinned at him and said, "Looks like the end of the road, Señor, or should I say, the end of a rope?" Brightenkamp started backing away, but by this time, Toady and two of Chaco's vaqueros had gotten around behind.

"Raise your hands, Señor, or I'll send this lead ball between your eyes," Chaco said. Instead of a verbal answer, Brightenkamp lowered his head and made a run toward Chaco. He waited until the last second and easily stepped to one side. The man hit the ground on his face but quickly got up, spitting dirt and trying to fight. Chaco didn't give him any room but started with both fists to tear his face from his head. They went on for several blows until Brightenkamp fell for the fourth time and made no move to get up. Finally, he raised a hand for a halt. He was totally beat. Chaco had only a few spots to show for the licks he took.

By that time most of the other rangers, vaqueros, and Em had gathered to watch the final few licks. Chaco got quite a lot of handshaking and such for his part. I think all of us were surprised that Chaco had beat him so easily and so badly. I was sure glad Chaco was on my side.

Oh, the other Germans in Brightenkamp's little army were all handcuffed from behind their backs, and several of Chaco's vaqueros, along with Em Taylor, had already headed east and south down to Del Rio. Bill Belcher's hands were on their way back to Brackett. That pretty well sums up what turned out to be a big day for most of us, especially Chaco and his ranch crew. Maybe they could get back to ranching.

Marshall Kip Mason waited 'til the others had left the room and sat down by my bed.

"Buck, you took quite a hit with that rifle, but lucky for you, the head was turned just right. We didn't know for two days if you'd make it or not."

"Two days? Was I out that long?"

"You sure were, and boy, are we glad to see you feeling better."

"Who said I was feeling better?"

"You will be when we get you back in circulation again. I 'spect a certain young lady at Rattlesnake Ranch is waiting to welcome you back."

Chaco and Toady came back in, followed by Captain Maxey. I told them all to get out and let me sleep and eat for a week. They did.

After a few days, Toady came in and told me, "Buck, we need to ride when you feel up to it. Let me help you out of bed." To my surprise, I made it okay. "See, Buck, if it had been anywhere else on your body, I don't think you could get up and around so quick."

"Me neither, my good friend. Take me out to my horse for a short ride."

Epilogue

I didn't get to ask Rosita about marriage again. I lost my nerve when it came time to talk to Chaco. Somewhere down the line I'm sure I'll regret it very much. With a heart full of sadness, I rode with the others back to Austin and vowed I would return to this area as soon as I could. Maybe I could buy the ranch we looked at and settle there. Only time would tell.